Waves of Light

Other Books in the Growing Faithgirlz!™ Library

Bibles

The Faithgirlz! Bible

NIV Faithgirlz! Backpack Bible

Faithgirlz! Bible Studies

Secret Power of Love

Secret Power of Joy

Secret Power of Goodness

Secret Power of Modesty

Fiction

From Sadie's Sketchbook

Shades of Truth (Book One)

Flickering Hope (Book Two)

Waves of Light (Book Three)

Brilliant Hues (Book Four)

Sophie's World Series

Sophie's World

Sophie's Secret

Sophie Under Pressure

Sophie Steps Up

Sophie's First Dance

Sophie's Stormy Summer

Check out www.faithgirlz.com

From Sadie's Sketchbook

Waves of Light

Book Three

Naomi Kinsman

ZONDERVAN.com/
AUTHORTRACKER
follow your favorite authors

ZONDERKIDZ

Waves of Light
Copyright © 2012 by Naomi Kinsman Downing

This title is also available as a Zondervan ebook.
Visit www.zondervan.com/ebooks

Requests for information should be addressed to:

Zonderkidz, 5300 *Patterson Ave SE, Grand Rapids, Michigan 49530*

Library of Congress Cataloging-in-Publication Data

CIP applied for: ISBN 978-0-310-72666-1

Editor: Kim Childress
Cover design: Cindy Davis
Interior design and composition: Greg Johnson/Textbook Perfect

Printed in the United States of America

12 13 14 15 16 /DCI/ 20 19 18 17 16 15 14 13 12 11 10 9 8 7 6 5 4 3 2 1

For my parents, who taught me to believe
in Christmas miracles, big and small.

Chapter 1

Scheming

I didn't bother waiting for Vivian to answer my knock. Instead, I threw open her front door and ran down the hall, past the tank of red and orange tropical fish, through the sunny kitchen, and into the back room, which smelled of oil paint and charcoal dust. Glow-in-the-dark constellations decorated the ceiling and one indigo-blue wall. The other walls were all windows overlooking the back porch and the forest beyond. Outside, clumps of leftover snow melted here and there, and wildflowers popped up, dots of purple and yellow in the otherwise spring green grass. Vivian and Frankie sat on stools pulled up to the paint-smeared table, already drawing.

"You're late, Sadie." Vivian gave me a stern look, but we all knew there were only two rules in her art studio.

One: Mistakes are to be expected. Two: Never give up.

I was the only person worried about my lateness today. I didn't want to miss a second of drawing time. I'd traded a few minutes of class for the final please, pretty please that had finally pushed Dad over the edge.

"He said I could go!" I gasped, still catching my breath.

Frankie vaulted off her chair and threw her arms around me. "Oh, Sadie! Thank you, thank you, thank you!"

I hugged her back, laughing. "So, what are we working on today?"

"More perspective." Frankie rolled her eyes. "I can't get my landscapes to line up. Something always ends up giant or miniature."

I peeked over Vivian's shoulder as she fussed over her sketch, adding a line here, erasing a line there. Yet another plan for a three-dimensional piece to include in the New York exhibit.

"I've never seen you nervous before—about anything." I dug through my backpack for my sketchbook.

"Usually I'm not. But then two schemers pitched my art—behind my back—to an art gallery."

"Oh come on, Viv. You know you're excited," Frankie said.

"And scared out of my mind. What will New York City art collectors think of my sculptures?"

Frankie grabbed Vivian's sketchbook and held it up like a hostess on the Home Shopping Network. "Ladies and gentlemen, check out these astounding works of art by the Amazing Vivian Harris. Buy them before they're gone!"

"I think the cookies just dinged," Vivian said, heading for the door.

"You could thank us," Frankie teased.

Vivian called over her shoulder, "Thank you!"

I grinned at Frankie. "She loves it."

"Setting up the art show was totally selfish," Frankie said. "I couldn't stand the thought of flying to New York by myself. Now that you're coming, at least the drive will be fun. If only there wasn't doom afterward."

"I love road trips." I climbed onto the stool next to her and grabbed a pencil. "Besides, your mom can't be that bad."

"Crystal glasses and high heels aren't my thing." Frankie jabbed her sketchbook with a pencil. "My mom hates my clothes—especially my favorite pair of boots. And she thinks not having a manicure is a disaster."

Frankie forced a smile, but her happy energy was gone. Joking around, planning for Vivian's art show, even driving to New York together—the facts still remained. Frankie's dad had decided to move to Canada, and her mom wouldn't let Frankie leave the country to go live with him. So, without having any say, Frankie had to move to New York.

"I've tried everything. Dad won't change his mind," Frankie said.

"Tell him my dad is leaving soon," I said. "That should help."

Frankie bit back a smile. "You don't know that."

"I'm pretty sure. Dad's done mediating now. And the hunters won't stand for any more bear regulations." And if the Department of Natural Resources needed any more community mediation, Dad wasn't likely to be their guy. Most of Owl Creek's hunters were convinced Dad had sided completely with Helen and her bear research. The DNR would have to hire someone else. For now, Dad was busy finishing up paperwork, and after that, he'd need a new job.

"There's always something. Maybe Helen's new research on how bear bluster isn't aggressive?" Frankie suggested.

"It's too late. The DNR already sent Patch to live at the zoo." Now I was the one jabbing my sketchbook with my pencil.

"Too late for Patch ... but that wasn't just bluster. She was a dangerous bear," Frankie said.

I didn't answer. This subject was one area that could turn into a knock-down, drag-out fight between Frankie and me, and I'd learned the hard way to keep my mouth shut. We'd never agree about the bears.

Vivian came back with a plate of peanut butter cookies. "Has it turned into World War Three in here?

"Not if there are cookies." I handed one to Frankie and took one for myself.

The gooey center melted on my tongue.

Vivian looked at Frankie's half-finished drawing and then at my scribble-scrabble page. "Looking a little dismal, girls."

I'd been in such a hurry to draw, but now I wasn't in the mood. I closed my sketchbook. "Can we help you get ready for New York, Vivian?"

Vivian sat back down with her plans. "I need to measure all of the sculptures so I can pencil out the display when I'm in the art gallery."

"I don't see why you can't just take everything with you when you go," I said.

"No way." Frankie took a second cookie. "If I have to move to New York, then I'm getting as many visits from Vivian as I can. And maybe you'll come back with her too, Sadie."

"We'll see. I think Dad's only letting me go because it's during spring break." Also it gave him time to deliver Mom to the health spa in California. And, of course, he wanted to distract me from hoping too much that this time Mom would finally get better.

"So just the statues outside?" Frankie asked. "Are there any others hiding inside?"

"No." Vivian handed Frankie a tape measure. "I put the pieces outside because the ceramic shards need sunlight to reflect properly. Inside light just doesn't cut it. At the gallery, I'll have to use theatre lighting."

"What do you want us to measure?" I asked.

"Height and circumference." Vivian frowned at a page in her sketchbook. "You're sure you don't want to draw? I hate to use up your drawing time."

"I'm all twitchy," I said. "I can't sit still."

"And if I have to draw this tree one more time, my head will explode." Frankie set her pencils down.

Vivian laughed. "Okay. Take the cookies. The fresh air will do you both good."

Statues peeked around tree trunks and stood guard between bushes along Vivian's gravel driveway. They weren't people, really, or creatures, but they had a magical, almost human quality to their curved arms and legs. None had distinct faces. Features, hair, fingers, clothing—these were all implied. So if you looked out along the path in the dark, you wouldn't know if you were looking at a line of living sentries or statues.

Frankie headed for the nearest one. "I thought they were creepy at first."

I opened Vivian's notebook to jot down the measurements. "What should we call this one?"

Frankie pointed to the winglike piece on its back. "Angel."

As we worked, I listened to the forest sounds—a bird call here, wind whispering through branches there. Suddenly, the bushes across the driveway rustled. Two pairs of fuzzy ears poked up above the green leaves, too big to be cubs, but too small to be full-grown bears. Trying not to move too suddenly, I pointed at the yearlings. Frankie watched warily, worried I knew, that a mother bear would be close behind. But no mother appeared, and soon the bears chased one another back the way they'd come.

Frankie let out her breath. "Well, that's one thing I won't miss. Bears sneaking up on me."

I rolled my eyes. "Yeah. One-year-old bears. Super scary."

"Ha-ha!" She grabbed a handful of snowy grass and shoved it down the back of my shirt.

"Hey!" I reached for some grass of my own just as Vivian came out onto the front porch.

"You girls just about done?" she called.

I showed Frankie the list, which covered only about half the statues in the yard.

"Umm . . ." Frankie answered. "We promise we'll be done measuring before we leave on Saturday."

"You girls," Vivian said. But I heard a smile in her voice.

The minute she closed the door, I ripped out another handful of grass and chased after Frankie, who ran shrieking and laughing. Measuring could wait until after I'd paid Frankie back.

Chapter 2

Promise

"Incoming!" Dad shouted as I opened the door, just seconds before Higgins made impact.

Higgins had grown into his full, chocolate-lab-sized self, and was big enough now to jump up and slam his paws into my chest. So of course, "Knock Down Sadie" had become his new favorite game. For some reason, he never did this to Mom, which was good, or to Dad, which was plain unfair.

"Ugh! What did he eat?" I rolled to the side, shielding my face from the dog's tongue.

When I'd finally freed myself, I wiped fishy slobber off my face. "Seriously. Someone needs to brush his teeth."

Dad poked his head out of the kitchen and tossed me a towel. "Did someone just volunteer for the job?"

Higgins trotted behind me into the kitchen, where spaghetti sauce and noodles bubbled on the stove, and garlic bread baked in the oven.

"Do you want to grate the cheese?" Dad asked. "Mom should be down any second."

"How's she feeling?" I asked.

"Worried. Not sure her suitcase is going to zip up." Dad winked and I grinned back.

Just like old times, back when Mom was truly herself. It had often taken Dad, me, and sometimes my best friend Pippa to sit on Mom's suitcase in order to zip it shut. The only thing Mom was more passionate about than organizing was packing.

"You never know what might happen when you travel," she'd say. "This way, we'll be ready—come what may."

I used to believe her suitcase was magical as I watched her shove every last shoe that she, Dad, and I owned—along with three umbrellas, enough snacks to feed an army, a flashlight, and binoculars, just in case—inside her luggage.

By the time I'd grated the cheese into a bowl and set the table for dinner, Mom had come downstairs. With her cheeks full of color, she looked better than she had in weeks. I fought against the way my insides inflated, hope growing like a balloon, filling me painfully full. Dad's face glowed too. And why shouldn't we hope? The spa doctors had promised to run a full round of tests, to look at Mom's diet and exercise habits and vitamin levels, and to help her build a real-life plan to feel better. No more miracle cures or drugs with horrible side effects. Chronic fatigue syndrome, the doctors explained, went deeper than any one medication or treatment plan.

Mom had been having so many ups and downs because she'd been treating only part of the problem. Making a body healthy required treating the whole body—physically, mentally, and spiritually. Two weeks at their spa, the doctors said, and Mom would be a brand-new person. Even now, with only the promise of feeling better, she had a spark I hadn't seen for months.

Please God, I whispered, *let this one finally work.*

Throughout dinner, we teased Mom about all the things she'd forgotten to pack. Then Dad brought out a tray of three chocolate cupcakes with sprinkles, each lit by a candle, for dessert.

"I picked them up at the bakery," he said. "Consider it your early Easter basket."

"Are you sure you'll be okay, Sadie?" Mom asked for the millionth time that week. "I mean, not being with us on Easter?"

"Look at her, Cindy. She can hardly sit still in her chair," Dad said, laughing. "We should be more worried about whether she'll come home from New York."

Higgins jumped up to sniff the remaining cheese on my plate.

"Down, Higgy." I pushed his paws away and bit into my cupcake. "Did you ask Helen and Andrew to watch Hig?"

"No. Since you'll see Andrew at youth group tomorrow, I figured we could ask him in person. Or Higgins could stay at the kennel."

Higgins flopped on the floor and sighed pathetically. *Kennel* wasn't his favorite word. I scratched his ears and then took a load of dishes out to the kitchen to wash and dry—my chore for the week. But I didn't mind this time because as I worked, Dad made a pot of coffee and took mugs out to the table. Then he and Mom sat, drinking and talking the way they used to.

Their voices rose and fell—a comfortable, happy sound. I slipped upstairs knowing they couldn't miss the noise, with Higgins panting and bounding as we climbed; but I didn't say anything to them. Talking would have broken the spell.

I caught Higgins by the collar before he leapt into my room. Cardstock, envelopes, glue sticks, cut-up magazines, and colored pencils littered my floor. An orderly mess, which I'd left mid-project before leaving for school that morning. Carefully, I guided Higgins on the only clear path through the piles. He jumped onto the bed, pawed the comforter into a perfect nest, and curled up.

Half the cards waited inside their envelopes, ready to be glued into the scrapbook. I would have finished the project last week, if it hadn't been for my crazy plan to use magazine letters of all shapes and sizes to describe the various scavenger hunt tasks. I'd finally found all of the letters, and now they lay across the final cards, ready to be pasted down.

I started on the next card:

Find a reflective surface and draw your own face.

Hopefully, Frankie would enjoy this scavenger hunt. At least we'd have a connection—I'd do the tasks, too, and send my drawings to Frankie so she could add them to the scrapbook.

When I'd first moved to Owl Creek, Pippa gave me a top-ten book that she'd made for me: reasons we'd always be best friends. Knowing it was there, waiting for me on my desk, had pulled me through those first frustrating weeks. Frustrating because of Frankie, actually. Funny how everything changed once we'd started taking art lessons with Vivian. The things we used to argue about didn't seem to matter much now.

Anyway, Frankie was right. She shouldn't have to move to New York against her will. But since I couldn't change her situation, I could at least try to distract her.

After a few hours of work, Dad knocked on my door. "'Night, Sades. Don't stay up too late."

I called back, "Okay, Dad. Love you."

My eyes were starting to droop, so I finished the last two words on the card. Slowly, the house became still. Somehow, it didn't feel right to take out my journal until everything was totally quiet. I stacked the letters and cards and art materials on one side of the room so Higgins wouldn't romp all over them in the night.

I hadn't emailed Pips for days because I'd been so busy with the scavenger hunt project. I powered on my email and prepared myself for the tirade. Pippa's emails didn't fail me. In fact, *tirade* didn't even begin to describe them. I sighed and started typing my response.

Pips, I know. I'm sorry you were worried. Frankie's scavenger hunt has totally taken over my life. But good news! Dad said I could go to New York … what should I wear? I'll be there for only a day and a half because Vivian has to hurry home to work on finishing the exhibit. It opens May 4, a month from today. While I'm in New York, we're going to paint a mural on Frankie's wall. We've been planning it for weeks, but now I get to help her with it.

It's weird. After not liking Frankie for so long — I'm really going to miss her.

You should have been here tonight. Remember when we used to play spy, and we'd sneak around while Mom and Dad drank coffee at the table? Remember how they got so into their conversation that we could sneak all the way to the table and they didn't even notice? Tonight was like that.

I'm scared because I'm starting to hope this is it — that Mom will get better. Do you think hoping too much might ruin her chances?

I closed my laptop. Inside my bedside table drawer, my journal and a rainbow of pastels and colored pencils waited. Since I'd started my nighttime ritual a few months ago, I hadn't missed a night. My thoughts settled as lines and shapes filled the journal pages. No one would have minded my need to draw, to send out questions and listen for whispered answers.

But I kept my ritual private anyway. Keeping the secret made it more special.

Tonight, I closed my eyes and pictured Mom's face, her eyes dancing with laughter at the dinner table. Once I could see every contour, I began drawing. I used to think prayers had to be elaborate with lots of important words or just the right requests; but as I continued to draw, night after night, something happened. Instead of talking *at* God, I started to feel like I was talking *with* him. Not through words, but through images.

Sometimes when I had questions, pictures I hadn't thought of on my own would appear on the page — as though my hand rested in God's, and his hand guided mine while I drew. Not like fortune-telling because I still didn't have any direct answers. Instead, I had new ideas, new questions, new possibilities to explore. The pictures seemed like questions — like God was asking: *Have you thought of it this way? Why not look here?*

Mom's face took shape, her eyes dark but hopeful, ready to believe she'd finally get better. As I drew, I found myself twining vines around her legs and arms. At first I thought they were binding her, but then I added flowers all over them. And as the flowery vines started growing beyond her fingers and sprouting from the tips of her hair, I realized she was actually *blooming*. Mom ... blooming. The drawing felt like a promise.

Chapter 3

Found

I can't believe you guys are going to New York without me." Ruth leaned against the VISITOR PARKING sign. "And you're deserting us for the Easter egg hunt."

"We're going to miss you, too." I stood on tiptoe and looked for Helen's car again. It should have pulled into the church parking lot ten minutes ago. "Where is Andrew?"

Behind us, the worship band struck their first chord. Ruth glanced that way.

"Let's go in." I laced my arm through hers. "Wouldn't want to miss any of Cameron's music."

Ruth rolled her eyes. "Like we didn't just wait forever on the curb for Andrew ..."

Ruth and I practically finished one another's sentences these days. Where Frankie and I carefully skirted certain subjects, Ruth and I fought it out whenever we disagreed. In that way she was an even closer friend than Pippa, and

I'd known Pips my whole life. I could tell Ruth anything. If she didn't agree with me, she'd tell me so. And if we had to, we'd simply agree to disagree.

We hurried across the grassy field toward the Tree House, newly painted for the spring. Even now, after coming here for youth group every week since September, the odd turrets and decks jutting out from the branches of the huge tree behind the church made me smile. Especially now, actually, because Penny's obsession with bright colors had migrated from her hair to the Tree House. Our youth group leader had gone wild, adding magenta trim around the windows and lime green accents across the deck railing. The snow was finally gone from the roof and branches, leaving all the weathervanes and whirligigs free to spin and ring. As we climbed the rope ladder, the tinkling of the chimes mixed with the deep beat of the bass drum. We slipped inside and found an open cushion on the nearest window seat.

Music washed over me the way it always did when the band played. Most people sang along, but I just listened as the voices wove together, filling the small space with an energy I wanted to be able to draw. Not being able to see something didn't mean it wasn't there.

Ruth's voice was like liquid gold, solid and smooth. Sitting by her was like having my own mini-concert. Yet for some reason, she refused to let Cameron, the leader of our youth group's student worship band, hear her sing — no matter how many times he asked. Her stubbornness made no sense to me.

As the song finished, the door opened and Andrew slipped into the room.

The corner of his mouth tipped up as he sat beside me. "Sorry," he whispered. "Phone call."

That smile. He'd flashed that same smile at me when I'd first seen him, surrounded by bears at the research station where he and his mom, Helen, lived. At first I'd assumed the bears were making my heart thud like a bowling ball against my ribcage. But even now, far away from the bears, Andrew had the same effect on me.

He nudged me with his elbow. "I hear you're going to New York instead of hiding Easter eggs in full view and chasing a crowd of very small people around the church lawn."

I elbowed him back. "You only volunteered so you can skim candy off the top."

He winked and happiness bubbled up inside me.

Doug bounded up to his usual stool at the front of the group, and Penny joined him. I could tell she was trying not to smile. Our youth leaders were up to something.

Doug rubbed his hands together. "So, we've had normal youth group for months, right?"

No one answered.

"Right?" he asked again.

"Right," we all echoed warily.

"And you all know that tomorrow's Good Friday. But you may not know about the vigil. All day long, people from church will be coming to the sanctuary to pray so at least one person is there at all times. If there's any way you can attend tomorrow, I encourage you to do so. Even if you can't come to the vigil, take time for some quiet this weekend — let God draw close to you."

"How do we *let* God do anything?" Claudia asked. "He's powerful enough to do whatever he wants."

"Right, but God doesn't force a relationship on us. He wants us to talk to him, to open up to him — the same way we might call a friend whenever we're thinking of that person."

When Claudia shrugged, Ruth elbowed me and smiled. Claudia constantly tried to catch Doug saying the wrong thing, so we secretly loved it when she backed herself into a corner.

"So what's going to be un-normal about youth group then?" Irritation filled Claudia's voice.

"Ah, yes." Doug motioned toward his coleaders. "Penny, Ben, and I were talking this week about all the cool things you guys have done as a group this year — particularly how you helped give Christmas to the Thompson family. Well, Maundy Thursday is also a time to give, and since tons of places around the world need aid, we've cooked up a plan."

"And the plan is . . . ?" Ted wasn't known for his patience.

Doug grinned. He was dragging out the reveal, and we all knew it. "We have so many talented people in our youth group —"

"Spit it out, Doug!" Ted shouted.

Doug threw up his hands as if in defeat. "Actually, Jasper should tell you about it. This was his idea, after all."

As Jasper shuffled to the front of the room, everyone razzed him about not saying something earlier.

"A few weeks ago," Jasper said, "I went to Canada to visit my aunt and uncle, and my family saw this play out in the forest. Each scene happened in a different part of the woods, and the audience hiked to get from scene to scene. So I asked Doug if we could do a play like that here—you know, to raise money for a good cause."

Hands shot up all over the room.

"What play?"

"Raise money for who?"

"When would we start?"

Doug laughed and held up his hands. "Whoa! Let's take this one step at a time. No decisions about the play or the cause have been made yet. Let's start there. Whoever wants to discuss possible play scripts, head over to the snack tables with Penny. If you want to brainstorm about good causes, meet with me over here at the windows."

Ruth and I decided to join Penny and Andrew headed for Doug's group.

"It should be a play that lots of people know," Claudia was saying. "Like *The Sound of Music* or something like that."

"But shouldn't it be one that takes place in a forest?" Lindsay asked.

Always dramatic, Bea threw her hands in the air and leaned forward. "Wait! What if we used improv games to turn a story into a play, like the way we created our

Christmas skit two years ago? No set script to start? We used an old Christmas story then, but this time we could use a folk tale or something."

"Oooh!" Ruth said. "How about that story Penny told us last Easter. Remember, Penny?"

"That was just—" Penny began.

"She wrote this story," Lindsay jumped in to explain, "that was like a folk tale, kind of. This girl got kidnapped and locked inside a music box. Then she escaped and there was this big storm—"

Penny shook her head. "I don't know ..."

"Come on, Penny. Please?" Bea asked.

Penny looked around the group. Clearly, she was outnumbered. "Fine. We can use my story. Using material we own, and not having to write a script ahead of time will make things easier, since we want to start rehearsals next week during spring break."

Ruth frowned and whispered to me, "You'll be gone part of next week."

"I'll talk to Penny. It'll be okay," I said.

After some debate, Penny and I decided I would head up the set crew, which suited me fine. Vivian could help me make some three-dimensional art pieces, a good challenge for me and different than just drawing images on a page.

When Doug gathered everyone together, the other group explained that they wanted to raise money to send food and clean water to children in Somalia. The vote was unanimous. We'd all seen the recent newscasts about the drought over there, and we wanted to help. Even Jasper, who usually wanted to help people locally—someone he could see with his own eyes—agreed this was the perfect idea.

Penny announced that play auditions would be held on Monday, and then Cameron and the band took the stage for one final song. They played "Amazing Grace" unplugged. As everyone sang, the excitement about everything to come—my trip to New York, Vivian's art show, designing sets for the play, even my hopes about Mom—they all settled like confetti drifting to the floor.

"I once was lost, but now am found; was blind, but now I see."

I'd felt lost for much of the past year. In the same way you suddenly realize after being sick for a long time that you finally feel better, I realized the words of this hymn were finally true for me. My life wasn't perfect or anything. I still had all kinds of questions. But here, sitting between Ruth and Andrew, filled with happiness, I didn't feel lonely or confused. Before, I'd often felt like someone pretending to be Sadie, or hoping to be Sadie someday—the Sadie I wanted to be. Now, I finally fit inside my own skin.

I'm right here. I'm found.

From: Sadie Douglas
To: Pippa Reynolds
Date: Thursday, April 5, 10:01 PM
Subject: Some girl

So I talked to Andrew after youth group, and he said he'd take care of Higgins while we're away. But then he told me the reason he was late tonight. He was on the phone with this girl, Annabelle, because she's coming to town. Her family is going to live at the research station for a few weeks, while they open up their summer house at the lake. Her dad runs this boating resort every summer. Ruth was all excited and so was Andrew. Every time he said Annabelle's name, his voice changed — like it was all melted chocolate or something. Who is Annabelle?

From: Sadie Douglas
To: Pippa Reynolds
Date: Friday, April 6, 6:22 PM
Subject: RE: Just ask him

We dropped off Higgins at Andrew's house tonight, and I tried to ask him about Annabelle. I really did. It's just that I got this lump in my throat every time he said her name. He couldn't stop talking about how much I'm going to like her, and how he's so glad she's coming early this year. Maybe I don't have to ask. Maybe it's obvious. He likes her, right?

He gave me an envelope and made me promise not to open it until Sunday. He said it's an Easter surprise. I know what you're thinking: Why would Andrew give me an Easter surprise if he's crazy about Annabelle, right? I don't know what to do, Pips.

Mom's all packed. She and Dad are leaving for California early in the morning. Vivian will pick me up around 10:30, so I have a little more time to pack tomorrow. I'm trying to be excited. And I am excited. If only I wasn't so worried about this Annabelle thing. Teaching Sunday school sounds fun, especially the part where you act out the stories with the kindergarteners. How long have you been going to church with your Grandma? Is your family going with you, too?

Chapter 4

Pictures in the Dark

We'd left midmorning for our drive to New York and had skipped lunch; by three, we were starving and needed to stretch our legs.

"Tacos or burgers?" Vivian asked us.

"Tacos," I answered.

"Burgers," Frankie said.

"We'll drive through both, then," Vivian said.

We collected our food and found a picnic table at a park. The cool breeze tickled my neck, and I didn't mind that my food was sloppy because we were eating outside. After we threw away our trash, Frankie and I went over to the swings and tried to swing as high as the bar.

"Vivian, I want to learn how to draw this. The air, I mean," I called out as I swung backward, my stomach dropping in that way that gives you shivers to the very roots of your hair. "You can feel it all around you, but you can't see it. I think you should be able to see it."

"What would it look like?" Frankie asked.

"I don't know. All different colors, like the way prisms make rainbows. But it would be all thick and shimmery — mixed together."

I wanted to hold on to this fluttery, happy feeling while Frankie was still around, Mom was on her way to getting healthy, and an unopened note from Andrew sat in my pocket. Right now, this minute — life couldn't get much better.

"Okay, girls. Time to hit the road," Vivian called.

We counted to three and then leapt from the swings. Vivian planned to drive until ten o'clock, and then we'd stay in a motel. We'd drive the rest of the way to New York in the morning. Frankie's mom had arranged for us to have a special Easter dinner, so we had to be in town by two o'clock at the latest.

When we finally parked at the motel, my legs felt like Jell-O. I dragged myself upstairs, and fell into bed.

"Uh-uh. No way I'm sleeping in the same bed as you if you don't brush your teeth first." Frankie dragged me to my feet and into the bathroom.

I half-slept through the teeth brushing and face washing and putting on of pajamas, and then I slipped into one side of the queen-size bed. Frankie took the other side, and Vivian took the rollaway bed. I was asleep before my head hit the pillow.

I awoke with a too-full feeling, thoughts pinging around inside my head like marbles knocking against one another. The room had an air-conditioner chill and smelled of strawberry-scented air freshener. My mind started to piece together where I was—not in my own room, but a motel room—dark, but not too dark.

A light illuminated the small desk by the door, and pencils scratched across paper, stroke after rhythmic stroke. I propped myself up on my elbow to watch Vivian draw. Her black hair fell loose around her shoulders, and she wore a polka-dotted tank top with striped pajama pants. So Vivian. So unlike every other adult I knew.

Carefully, so I wouldn't wake Frankie, I slid out of bed and tiptoed across the room.

"What are you drawing?" I whispered.

Vivian looked surprised, as though I'd pulled her from a dream. "Did I wake you?"

"I think I woke myself. My head is too full." I'd been so tired that I hadn't done my nightly drawing, and now I was a mess.

Vivian gestured at her sketchbook. "Well, you know what I do when my head is too full."

Vivian had drawn a series of pictures of her house in every season. Fall—a few leaves strewn on the ground and a pumpkin resting on her porch. She sat on the porch swing with a steaming mug in her hand. Winter at night—piles of snow, a little boy facing a snowman in the yard, and bright stars in the moonless sky. Spring—Vivian in her front yard, finishing the angel sculpture, a few patches of snow still here and there. And then summer—the raspberries in full bloom, a reddish sunrise streaking across the sky, Vivian holding hands with a man. I guessed her husband, David, who'd died a few years ago.

"New York seems so over the top for me, the kind of thing I've always dreamed about," Vivian said. "But what actually makes me happiest is my own home full of memories."

"Is that Peter?" I pointed to the little boy.

"Yes." Vivian smiled. "He asked about you the other day. Wanted to know how you were."

I sat down on the rollaway bed. "What did you tell him?"

"That you're becoming quite the artist. And, as always, you are such a kind friend."

"Not such a kind friend to him." I pulled at a loose stitch in the blanket.

"Peter might have stayed with me forever trying to help me get over David. But I will never get over my husband. You gave my son a gift. He's free now, fighting fires and living his own life. Even though facing the charges from the DNR was difficult, Peter grew from the experience. You told the truth, Sadie. And the truth always helps people become free."

Tears pooled in my eyes. I didn't want to cry, so I just nodded and blinked hard. I hadn't expected to talk about Peter. He hadn't even been on my list of worries for the day. Now I really wanted to draw, but I wanted privacy to do it. This kind of drawing wasn't something I liked to do with anyone watching me. Vivian may have sensed my hesitation, or maybe she really was tired. In either case, she closed her sketchbook.

"I think I'll lie down now," she said. "But feel free to leave the light on for a while, if you want. It won't bother me."

She slipped into the rollaway bed, and I glanced over to make sure Frankie was still asleep too. Sure enough, she was mouth-hanging-open, arm-draped-off-the-bed, deep asleep.

As quietly as I could, I unzipped the front pocket of my suitcase and took out my sketchbook and pencils. I returned to the desk and sat there, rolling my pencil between my fingers and studying the blank page in the lamplight, waiting for my heart to slow. My thoughts still clacked around, stirred up further by our conversation about Peter. Recently, ever since I'd moved to Owl Creek, actually, I'd felt like a human wrecking ball.

On the whole, things had gotten better for me. But still, so many people's lives had changed because of things I'd done or said. Peter, for one, had moved away from Owl Creek after I'd reported him for illegal hunting and the DNR revoked his hunting license for two years. Now Frankie was moving away because her dad couldn't stand my dad. Even though that wasn't exactly my fault, I felt guilty by association. And then Mom—while I knew her sickness wasn't my fault, I couldn't help but wonder if I could do something to help her get better. Should I help around the house more? Not ask her to drive me places? Was it possible to never worry her? And if I could somehow, miraculously, become the perfect daughter, would she finally get better?

I didn't know what to draw. I wanted to believe I was worried over nothing. I wanted to believe what Vivian had said—that Peter *needed* to move away, that I hadn't ruined his life or hers. I wanted to believe Frankie would eventually love living in New York. And I really, really wanted to believe the health spa would fix Mom. Finally. But wanting those things didn't erase my worries.

The blank page stared back at me. I finally drew a long black stroke right in the center of the page, winding around and around on itself. The line was too raw there, a tangled mess. I wanted to put it somewhere safe, somewhere hidden. I drew a box around it and added a padlock. Then I sketched waves and seaweed until the box sat at the bottom of the ocean.

I closed my eyes. The drawing wasn't finished. I'd locked up my mess and buried it, but I didn't feel at all settled. The air conditioner hummed, the desk light buzzed softly, and as I listened, an image floated into my mind. A key with an ornate handle, the kind that might come with a fancy diary, or the kind you'd find in an antique shop. A key to unlock secrets. I opened my eyes and stared at my picture. I didn't want to unlock that box. Keeping the box locked was the whole point of sinking it to the bottom of the ocean. But even with my eyes open, I could still see the key. It wasn't going away. Finally, because I knew I had no other choice, I drew a rock and put the key underneath.

That's good enough, isn't it? For the time being?

No answer boomed down from the sky—it never

did—but still, a velvety calm came over me. Words from one of Doug's talks came to mind. He'd said something like, "God gives us only what we can handle, never more." For a second or two, I thought I understood what Doug meant. Of course, I had more to think about, more to see, more to unlock. But for now, knowing about the box and the key was enough.

I closed my sketchbook and checked the clock before turning off the desk lamp. Twelve fifteen.

Happy Easter.

Chapter 5

Butterfly Sunrise

The alarm went off at five a.m., and we dashed around the motel room, pulling on clothes and packing up our stuff. Vivian wanted to find a little church to attend because it was Easter Sunday. I offered to Google something on Vivian's iPhone on the way, but she refused.

"How hard can it be to find a tiny church with stained-glass windows and a steeple?"

She seemed more concerned about how the church looked than the service, but I didn't say so out loud.

We piled into Vivian's pickup truck; drove through McDonalds for breakfast sandwiches, OJ, and coffee for Viv; and then we were off, back on the highway. As I'd expected, the roadway wasn't peppered with white, steepled churches. But since it wasn't even seven o'clock yet, we still had time to find Vivian's perfect church. I closed my eyes and the truck's motor lulled me to sleep.

When the truck stopped, I jerked awake. "What's going on?"

I didn't need to ask, really. We'd just pulled into a full parking lot next to a white, steepled church with stained-glass windows — exactly what Vivian had wanted.

The church sign read: BUTTERFLY SERVICE, 9 A.M.

"Not Easter service?" I asked.

Frankie shrugged as we walked up the steps and through the front door. Once, she'd called me "churchy." And then a few months later, she'd started going to youth group with me. So she wasn't totally opposed to churches. But this place, with its wooden pews and kneeling pads, was a little foreign — even for me.

People stood in the aisles and all around the room, hugging one another and complimenting the kids on their Easter dresses, suits, and even hats. Frankie and I had worn comfortable driving clothes, and our jeans and tennies were a little out of place. Vivian had planned ahead, though, and she was wearing a long moss-colored dress.

We slipped into a pew after shaking a few hands and explaining that, no, we weren't from around here, we were actually on our way to New York, and we'd wanted to find an Easter service to attend on the way. The knowing smiles from the regulars started to make me nervous.

They all said something along the lines of, "Well, this will be a treat for you, then."

What did they mean, exactly? That church would be a treat for us? Or that something during the service would be a treat?

Before I could worry too much, the organ launched into the "Hallelujah Chorus," and everyone stood as the music rumbled through the church. When the song ended, a bright-eyed woman came out in a white robe. She introduced herself as Janie, the head pastor.

Janie told the Easter story in her own words. And then she talked about transformation — how when someone goes through a period of darkness, she comes out on the other side of it changed and can't go back to the person she was before. I thought about the box and the key in my drawing the night before, and I wondered where I was — still in the darkness or on the other side?

"Life is a series of transformations," Janie said. "Just when we think we've finally changed for good, we learn there's more."

She explained that we go through the deepening process many times during a lifetime. Since God sent his Son to the world to walk among us and to sacrifice for us, Jesus had become like a bridge, fully human and fully God at the same time. Jesus knew all the unknowable things that God knew, but he also understood what it was like to be human, the pain and the joy. Maybe we couldn't connect with God very easily because God was so beyond our comprehension. But because Jesus had actually walked with us we could talk to him, and he could help us along the road to deepening.

Someone I could connect with. Yes. That was how I felt. I liked Janie and the way she put things. Words bubbled out of her, full of joy and something more — truth, I guess. She didn't seem to be talking about an idea she'd read about once. Her voice echoed with knowing, like she'd gone through darkness of her own. I wished I could talk with her more.

After she finished speaking, the choir led the congregation in a few more hymns, some of which Cameron's band had played during youth group. But the music sounded totally different when accompanied by an organ and the choir. "Joyful, Joyful We Adore Thee" was the final song of the service. I read the lyrics in the hymnal as the congregation sang:

> *Hearts unfold like flowers before You, opening to the sun above.*
> *Melt the clouds of sin and sadness; drive the dark of doubt away;*
> *Giver of immortal gladness, fill us with the light of day!*

I looked for the songwriter's name. Henry J. Van Dyke. He had to be an artist. The words were like drawings come to life with notes and rhythm. As the song finished, Janie brought out an armful of baskets filled with banded white boxes. She handed a basket to each usher, and they distributed the boxes down the rows.

Once she made it to the back of the church, Janie called, "Everyone have one?"

"Yes!" they all shouted back, like it was a well-rehearsed game.

"Well, come on, then." She threw open the doors and bounded down the front steps, her robe billowing behind her.

"What's going on?" Frankie asked.

Vivian shook her head. "No idea. Let's go find out."

We followed everyone outside. From the top of the steps, I looked down over the bright green lawn filled with kids, parents, and grandparents each one holding a white box. Janie counted to three and then took the band off her box, lifting the lid. The others did too, and suddenly the air was on fire with reds and yellows and oranges.

Eyes wide, I turned to Frankie. "Butterflies."

She nodded and whispered her own count to three. We opened our boxes, and our butterflies joined the fluttering of wings. They swirled in the air, lifted along by the wind.

"You wanted to draw air, right?" Frankie asked.

Now it was my turn to nod. I could hardly wait to get back into the truck with my sketchbook and draw a heart unfolding like a flower, the clouds of gloom melting away, and the air filled with a butterfly sunrise.

Chapter 6

Georgiana

By the time Vivian pulled up to Frankie's mom's brownstone in New York, my neck was stiff and my back ached from sitting too long. Vivian circled the block once to find a parking spot, but none of us felt very patient. So she gave up and parked in a nearby pay lot almost right away. We lifted our suitcases out of the truck and rolled them down the sidewalk.

Along the street, stairs and iron railings led up to doors with old-fashioned paned windows. Individual mailboxes and flower boxes gave the street a neighborhood feel, but at the end of the block, cars rushed by constantly with horns honking. Frankie's lips pressed together, and her shoulders stiffened with every step. I couldn't understand her reaction. The city buzzed with energy, full of possibilities. Wasn't she even the tiniest bit excited to live here?

We found the right set of stairs, and Vivian rang the buzzer. Immediately, we heard footsteps clicking, as though Frankie's mom had been perched inside, watching for us.

"Chase, they're here!" Her words glided musically up and down the scale.

"Boyfriend," Frankie mouthed to me just before the door swung open.

Frankie's mom threw open her arms sending ripples through the glittery silver scarf draped over the shoulder of her entirely black outfit.

"Francesca!" she said, her voice deep and husky like a movie star in a black-and-white movie. "You're finally here."

She swooped Frankie into a big hug, which Frankie couldn't have returned even if she'd wanted to because her arms were now pinned to her sides. After a long squeeze, Frankie's mom kissed her on both cheeks and then turned to Vivian and me. I backed up a step, not ready to be kissed by a woman I'd never met. But, with practiced grace, Frankie's mom merely extended a hand toward Vivian—the perfect hostess.

"I'm Georgiana. Delighted to meet you! Thank you so much for driving Frankie down here." She let go of Vivian's hand and smiled at me. "And you must be Sadie. I've heard so much about you. Well, don't just perch on the stoop. Come inside."

I followed Frankie and Vivian inside and instantly felt shabby in my jeans and sweatshirt as I pulled my battered suitcase with the wobbly wheel that squeaked. The house was white-glove clean, but artsy too.

"I'll give you the full tour in a minute. But for now, you must be thirsty. Come into the kitchen. Leave your bags here. Chase will take care of them."

She swept down the hallway, and we followed in her wake. Frankie shot me a "See?" look. I shrugged. Her mom was a bit over the top, but she was nice, too. At least she wasn't sagging in a chair because she didn't have the energy to stand up. Like my mom.

Georgiana kept up an endless stream of chatter as she guided us to three stools at the stainless-steel bar in the stainless-steel kitchen. The whole room was metal. If you wanted to, you could probably close the hall door and just spray down the counters and floors with a hose.

"We have goat cheese and edamame crackers. Oh, and blueberries. Those are an antioxidant, you know." Georgiana arranged the food on little white plates and handed us each a napkin. "Help yourself. I also have sparkling water: blackberry, lemon, or lime."

When she paused for a breath, Vivian answered, "I'll take blackberry, thank you."

"Me too," I added, and elbowed Frankie.

But Frankie was too late. Her mom had already launched a new stream of chatter.

"This house has been here for more than a hundred years, but Chase had it entirely remodeled. We left exposed brick in the other rooms; but here, we wanted cooking and cleaning to be simple—and what's more simple than steel?" She handed me my glass, and eyed Frankie. "Francesca, would you like some water?"

Frankie nodded, and that's when I realized she hadn't said a word since we'd walked inside. Maybe this was the problem. Her mom was like a tornado, and she couldn't get a word in edgewise.

"Don't eat too much." Georgiana took a tiny nibble from her cracker. "We're going to Waldy's for pizza tonight." To Vivian she added, "Don't worry, it's thin crust. Not as many calories. We figured the girls might enjoy something familiar for their first night in New York."

After a long pause during which I felt like someone had better say *something*, Frankie finally spoke. "But it's Easter."

"I know, darling," Georgiana said. "That's why pizza's so perfect."

No one explained why pizza was perfect. No one asked either.

"Well, here they finally are," a man's voice said from behind us.

I smelled him before I saw him. He smelled like the trendy stores that pumped cologne through their vents to bewitch mall shoppers to come spend money. This must be Chase, the boyfriend. He had dark curly hair and olive skin, and there wasn't a spec of lint on his three-piece suit.

"Chase, darling." Frankie's mom hugged him and kissed him on both cheeks.

"Georgiana." He lifted her up until her feet left the ground and twirled her around in a circle. I'd never seen anyone do that except in the movies.

I couldn't, not even for a second, imagine Georgiana with Frankie's dad. Why would two such opposite people get married? Georgiana introduced Chase to us, and then she launched into her next monologue about how much Vivian would love the art studio, how she couldn't wait to show it to her tomorrow, and how she was excited about our plans for the mural in Frankie's room. She didn't ask a single question, though, just told us how wonderful it would all be.

Once we'd eaten, Georgiana led us on a tour of the house, with its priceless—and strange—artwork, distressed plank floors, mood lighting, and plants that looked like they might want to eat you. While we toured, Chase brought our bags up to our rooms.

We ended the tour in Frankie's room, which had beige everything: walls, comforter, area rug.

"Neutral. It's the perfect canvas for your mural." Georgiana pointed to the long empty wall. "We can't wait to see what you'll do." Again, she pulled Frankie into a death-squeeze hug and said to Vivian, "We're so proud of our little artist. Now, let me show you to the guest room. Girls, we'll head out for dinner in about twenty minutes. Why don't you freshen up in the WC?"

After they left, Frankie opened the bathroom door and gestured as though she were presenting me with a luxury hotel room. "The WC, my lady."

I pressed my hand to my mouth to hold back the giggles and tiptoed inside. The bathtub was the size of a small hot tub, and the sink looked more like an ice sculpture than a sink.

"Ugh. How am I supposed to do this?" Frankie sat on the edge of the bathtub.

"Give it a chance, Frankie." I turned on the water and pumped foamy lavender suds onto my hands. "You might get used to washing your hands with Essence of Violet."

She rolled her eyes and waved her hand in front of her face. "Eeesh. Turn on the vent. That stuff is strong."

I shoved my dripping hands directly under her nose, and she pushed me away, laughing.

"Come on. We've got to freshen up."

"Whatever that means," Frankie said.

We quickly washed our faces and hands, and then we brushed our teeth and hair. After I'd changed into a less-rumpled top, I made Frankie put on some lip gloss. Before joining the others, we inspected ourselves in the mirror.

"Okay?" I asked Frankie.

"Okay." She nodded. "I have to admit, pizza does sound good."

I couldn't help adding, "And you won't have to think of a thing to say."

Frankie laughed. "No, darling. I sure won't, will I?"

We giggled all the way downstairs.

From: Sadie Douglas
To: Pippa Reynolds
Date: Sunday, April 8, 8:21 PM
Subject: RE: Bunny Suit Disaster

Frankie let me borrow her computer so I could email you back. We both almost wet our pants when I read your story about wearing the bunny suit inside the bounce house, falling down, and not being able to get back up. I wish I could have seen those kids trying to help you up while the others dogpiled you. Where were the other Sunday school teachers??!?

We went out for pizza tonight—real New York pizza that's baked in a stone oven. The whole place smelled like tomato sauce and cheese were baked into the walls. The restaurant has been around forever, I guess, and old black-and-white photos of movie stars and mobsters and former U.S. presidents lined the walls.

I'm worried about Frankie. She doesn't talk much around her mom. I guess it's because her mom is always talking. But she's constantly trying to "improve" Frankie, too, like telling her to watch her posture, stop picking at her fingernails, and not slurp her soda. Frankie's under constant surveillance. And her mom calls her "Francesca." Can you imagine calling Frankie, Francesca? I couldn't understand why Frankie didn't want to come to New York, but now I see the problem. I think her mom will try to change her into something she's not. And Frankie's mom is all mushy with her boyfriend, too. Which is kind of gross. They even rubbed noses during dinner.

I opened Andrew's card today. He gave me a necklace—and the pendant is a burst of three shooting stars. His note said: "Thought of you when I saw this … Happy Easter."

What does that mean? And what about Annabelle?

Chapter 7

Footprints

It wasn't until we were sitting there on the drop cloth, our toes dripping with glow in the dark paint, that Frankie and I realized the flaw in our plan. All the way across the room from the bathroom, we were trapped.

"Whose idea was this, anyway?" Frankie asked.

"You have to admit," I said, "The footprints are the perfect touch."

We sat back and studied our mural. Pine, maple, and aspen trees filled a twilight version of our forest back home, with wildflowers blooming in splashes of color, and stars bright against the darkening sky. Despite her mixed feelings about the bears, Frankie let me add Patch and her yearlings to the mural. Patch's ears and snout poked around the side of a thick tree, while her yearlings balanced in the branches above. After adding an owl, a red-feathered cardinal, a few hummingbirds, a raccoon, and a rabbit or two, we decided the mural needed something more.

"Something mysterious," Frankie had said.

Since we'd bought glow-in-the-dark paint for the stars, it seemed wasteful to use it for only a few stars and a sliver of moon.

"What about some footprints? Glow-in-the-dark ones. They could go down here in the darkest part of the forest so you wonder who left them and where they're going," I'd said.

Then we'd quickly torn off our socks and shoes, covered our feet with paint, and awkwardly angled ourselves until we could make the footprints go in the right direction, never considering how we'd wash our feet afterward.

I lay back now, careful not to touch the hardwood floor. "Looks like we'll be here for a while."

Frankie lay back too and sighed. "When you leave New York, this will all be so real and so horrible."

"What? Patch lurking in your bedroom — ready to sneak up on you during the night?"

Frankie laughed. I laughed too and the sadness dissolved for the moment. We couldn't avoid it forever, but I wasn't ready for good-byes yet.

"We could crawl to the bathroom," I suggested, pushing up onto my hands and knees.

Frankie held up her paint-coated hands and gave me a questioning look.

"So blow on them," I said.

Frankie smeared her hands down the back of my shirt,

so I dipped my fingers into the paint to pay her back. In the end, we lay down on the drop cloth again, giggling madly. It felt like all we'd been doing was laughing, as though laughter could keep everything else far away.

"I have a present for you," I said when we could finally breathe again.

I hadn't planned on telling her about it because I'd wanted to surprise her. But somehow, this felt like the right moment to say something about the scavenger hunt I'd planned.

"If you put another fake spider in my hair, you will pay," she said.

I grinned, remembering her manic dance as she'd tried to untangle the sticky legs from her hair. "At least it wasn't a real spider."

"If it had been ..."

I interrupted her. "It's a real present this time. But I'm not giving it to you until I leave."

"And you're not going to tell me what it is."

"So you'll have something to look forward to."

Downstairs, the chimes rang as the front door opened. "Francesca, are you home?"

"Ugh," Frankie said. "Already?"

"Francesca?" Her mom clacked upstairs and into the bedroom on impossibly teetery heels. "Girls, you're a mess! And we need to leave in fifteen minutes to make it to the gallery opening. Vivian's already there."

"What opening —" Frankie started to say, but her mom cut her off.

"Vivian will see the gallery in full regalia, so she knows what to expect next month." She stopped, looking pointedly at our feet. "What are you doing?"

"Mom, Vivian and Sadie are leaving tomorrow. Early."

Frankie's mom helped us to our feet, careful not to touch any of the wet paint. "All the more reason to have a night on the town, darling. Wait here. I'll get you some old socks so you can dash to the WC and wash off."

We wrestled socks onto our sticky feet and hurried into the bathroom, where we peeled out of our clothes and took turns rinsing off in the shower.

Frankie's mom knocked on the door. "Hurry, girls. We're late."

As Frankie toweled off, she rolled her eyes. "Honestly, we wouldn't want the chauffeur to have to wait."

After a few more mad minutes of dressing and brushing our hair and swiping on some lip gloss, we were as ready as we'd ever be. We followed her mom down to the car, and I slid into the backseat. Frankie's mom had studied the mural while we got ready, and now she analyzed our style and technique while Frankie bristled silently beside me. She hadn't asked for her mom's opinion. I stared out the window, trying to catch my breath.

After Frankie had come home from her trip to New York at Thanksgiving, I hadn't understood her reluctance to live with her mom. New York was the center of the art world, and I knew her mom spoiled her rotten. Now that I was here, though, I saw how out of place Frankie was. It was like watching a fish try to do ballet on dry land. But Georgiana didn't stop moving long enough to notice. Which was worse: a mom who was too exhausted to notice anyone but herself, or a mom who was too caught up in her own life to pay attention to you?

Women in black dresses, glittery heels, and perfectly manicured nails filled the brick and glass gallery. Frankie's mom swept us around the room and introduced us to Delores and Diamanté and Diandra. I'd never remember the names, and neither, I assumed, would Frankie.

After two hours of being petted and cooed over, my feet ached and my cheeks burned from smiling too hard for too long.

"Nothing like having a pet," Frankie whispered when her mom turned away to clink glasses with the gallery owner. "Want some fresh air?"

I nodded and followed her out to the gallery's front steps. Frankie sat and dropped her head into her hands.

"I can't do this. I can't be this person," she said.

"I didn't think I'd ever fit in when we moved to Owl Creek," I said.

"That's because I was doing my best to make you as miserable as possible."

I grinned. "Think of everything you'll learn about art here."

"Vivian can teach me what I need to know. Anyway, you saw those paintings in there, and the way everyone took them so seriously." She imitated one of the black-dress women. "See that red circle? The ragged edge portrays violence and betrayal. It just ... speaks." Frankie lowered her voice for this final word, a perfect imitation of the woman we'd overheard.

I choked back laughter. "I wish I had your present here. I can't wait for you to open it."

"Can't you just stay with me?" Frankie asked.

I took a deep breath trying to shape the thought that had been trying to come out — the thought I knew Frankie needed to hear — into words that would make sense. "Okay, don't laugh at me."

Frankie must have heard the change in my voice because she turned to face me. "I won't laugh. Promise."

"I don't think I would have started drawing if hadn't come to Owl Creek."

"But you already—"

"Not like I did once I met Vivian. Drawing pulled me closer and closer to seeing ..."

"Seeing what?" Frankie asked, as the silence stretched long.

My heart thudded against my ribcage as I tried to push out the words I'd known I would have to say at some point. I couldn't quite force myself to speak.

"Come on, Sadie. I promised I wouldn't laugh," Frankie said.

"God," I finally said. The name tumbled out of my mouth and fell between us as heavy as a stone. I was too afraid to look at her, too afraid to see her expression. My feelings were too private to talk about, but I knew Frankie needed to hear about my experience. As her friend, I had to tell her — no matter what she thought of me afterward.

I pushed on, faster now, filling the silence with words. "When I drew, I felt something bigger than me, tugging at me. I probably always believed in God deep down, but I didn't think about him much until I came to Owl Creek and all those bad things happened. It wasn't only that I realized God exists, but I discovered he cares. I mean, when you really look at a snowflake and pay attention to all the fine details, you can't help but see how much God must care. About everything. About us."

When I finally looked up, Frankie made an impatient gesture, worse than if she had laughed. "So you think bad stuff should happen to everyone? So God can prove he cares?"

"No. I just think ... I think when hard stuff happens, you realize you have help. Bigger help than you knew you had, and I think God's help really matters. That's all. It helps you keep going."

Frankie silently picked at her fingernail for a long time, and my heart felt like it was growing, expanding so much that soon it wouldn't fit inside my body. I couldn't catch my breath.

"I don't know if I believe in God, Sadie," Frankie finally said. "But I'll try to believe you — that something bigger out there is watching and helping. I really hope that's true."

We sat there watching clouds drift across the night sky,

white against the orange city glow, until Frankie's mom burst through the door behind us.

"Oh, Francesca, Sadie! I've been looking everywhere for you two. We should be getting home now."

For once, Frankie didn't make a snide comment. She must be exhausted. I'd leave her present on her bed in the morning, and hopefully she wouldn't wake up. I wanted her to have that surprise, at least—a small moment of happiness even though she'd be here on her own.

Chapter 8

Gone

My mouth tasted like moldy socks, my eyes were sticky at the corners, and I couldn't feel anything in the lower half of my left leg, which seemed to be tucked up under my knee. Why was I sleeping sitting up? I blinked my eyes and cradled my foot as what felt like millions of bees woke up under my skin, stinging me until my eyes watered.

"You okay?" Vivian asked from the seat next to me.

"My leg's asleep." I had to lift it off the seat with my hands to straighten it, and then I pressed my foot against the floor so the pain would hurry up and get over already.

"Lovely hair," Vivian handed me a steaming thermos. "It's hot chocolate. Should help wake you up."

Slowly, as the fog cleared from my head, I remembered getting into Vivian's truck. I must have fallen asleep immediately after we'd left Frankie's house. "How long have we been driving?"

"About four hours. It's nine thirty now."

I held the thermos in both hands and directly under my nose so the chocolate steam battled the terrible taste in my mouth. Finally, when I was sure I wouldn't drool all over myself, I took a sip.

Outside, puffy clouds hung in the bright blue sky, and the highway stretched on endlessly. Trees covered low hills on either side of the road, but other than the occasional semi-truck and a car or two, there were no signs of civilization.

"We're in Pennsylvania, a little way outside of Bellefonte," Vivian said. "We can stop and grab some breakfast."

"I need to brush my teeth."

Vivian gave me a sideways glance. "No kidding."

I leaned back and closed my eyes, still trying to wake up. Leaving Frankie's house was a foggy memory, almost like a dream. I'd tiptoed into Frankie's room and put the box at the foot of her bed. Maybe by now she was awake and reading the letter I'd written and rewritten until I was sure I'd gotten it just right.

Frankie,

Remember, whatever you do ... keep drawing. Vivian and I came up with some art assignments for you to do since we can't see you in person. Open one envelope every other day or so. Then send me your drawing, and I'll send you mine. Deal?

Love, Sadie

A small hollow space opened up inside me—a space that couldn't be filled by sending drawings back and forth. But if I felt this sad, how must Frankie feel? At least I had Ruth and Andrew and the play to go home to.

I opened my eyes. "How long will Frankie put up with being called Francesca?"

"Doesn't really fit her, does it?"

"None of it fits her."

"Well, her mom is an artist. Don't forget that." Vivian pointed to a restaurant sign up ahead. "Breakfast?"

"Yes, I'm starved." And my fingers itched to draw. I'd skipped drawing again last night. "It doesn't seem like Georgiana is an artist, at least not the way you are."

"There's more to her than what's on the surface." Vivian took the next exit. "When she showed me around the gallery, she surprised me, actually. Unfortunately, what's on the surface is terribly distracting. Frankie will have to get through a few layers before she really gets to know her mom."

"And you think she will?" I asked.

"If she keeps drawing, she can't help but see some different angles to her mom."

We turned onto Main Street, which was lined with trees that hung over the road. It reminded me of a postcard of some long-ago small town. As we drove underneath them, I looked up into the branches covered in brand-new leaves, thinking of the first task in Frankie's scavenger hunt:

Find something that doesn't look the same from two different angles.

From this point of view, the leaves were green lace against a blue sky. Maybe I'd draw the leaves from two angles—first drawing, done.

"I left the scavenger hunt on Frankie's bed this morning," I said.

Vivian smiled. "She'll love it."

We found a small coffee shop and ate egg sandwiches. Then we brushed our teeth in the small bathroom. Luckily, it was a one-person kind with a lock on the door, so no one came in while we spat our toothpaste into the sink. With food in my stomach and my dragon breath cured, I felt more like myself. I wet down and re-braided my hair, splashed cold water on my face, and headed out to the truck.

Back on the road, we played through Vivian's road trip playlist from start to finish—a full two hours. Now it was noon. On and on and on the road stretched. The trip back to Michigan would take seventeen hours; so if we were lucky, we'd be home by ten o'clock.

I jiggled my legs and shifted into a more comfortable position.

"Bored?" Vivian turned down the music.

"Kind of. I'm thinking about our youth group's play. I'm in charge of the sets."

"Do you know what you're making?"

"No idea. I haven't read the story yet. But I'm hoping you'll have time to help me with it. I mean, unless you're swamped with the exhibit."

"I'm sure we can work something out. Do you have a crew?"

"Not yet, but Penny said she'd ask for a parent volunteer or two. She doesn't want me to work the saw, for one thing. And there's some building stuff I don't know about. Like how to make something strong enough for an actor to stand on."

"We can look over the drawings together," Vivian said. "I'm better with chicken wire and cement, but I know a thing or two about wood."

Vivian pulled off the highway at a rest stop.

When we were back in the truck, Vivian let me look through her art show sketches. I flipped through the plastic-covered pages, and then napped until two. By then, we could no longer ignore our growling stomachs. We drove through Wendy's, because we'd already done McDonalds and Taco Bell. Since we were both impatient to get home, we ate in the truck and kept driving. Dad should be home from the airport by the time we got there. He'd spent a few days at Mom's spa, so he should have some news. I knew my imagination was running wild. I pictured Mom running on the beach with her hair swinging across her back and her cheeks flushed from the exercise. The way she used to be. I'd already banished all of my recent memories of her, pale as porcelain and draped limply across a chair or bed. I'd decided she would finally be better, no question. I knew disappointment was possible, but I couldn't help hoping. Something had to work. Mom couldn't live the rest of her life this way.

"You know, I think I can use a number of the sculptures from the yard," Vivian said, interrupting my thoughts. "I'm actually thinking the display should be like the yard back home, with the creatures and sculptures all tucked away between trees. Which means I'll have to create some trees, too."

Vivian went on about three-dimensional art and how she planned to use light to mirror sunrise and sunset in the room, making it as close to an outdoor forest as she could. When our stomachs started growling, we found a café, stretched our legs and then loaded up for the final part of the drive.

I fell asleep for a few minutes, but woke up as the sun started to set. My first thought was of Mom. I wanted so much for her to be okay that I couldn't concentrate on anything. I flipped through my sketchbook and did a loose sketch of the leaves, but I quickly lost interest. At least the sketch was a reminder so I could draw them properly after I got home. I played DJ for a while, scrolling through Vivian's playlist until we started to see familiar surroundings.

Vivian's cell phone buzzed.

"Answer that for me, will you?" she asked.

I dug through her purse and pulled out the phone, disappointed when the number on the screen wasn't Dad's. "Hello?"

"Hello, is this Vivian? Vivian Harris?"

"No, this is Sadie. Vivian is driving."

"Can you ask her to pull over?"

I didn't like this voice, clipped and official. The kind of voice that brings bad news.

"She's asking us to pull over."

Vivian frowned but pulled the truck onto the shoulder and turned off the engine.

She took the phone from me. "Hello?" Pause. "Yes, this is she." Long pause. Then all the color drained from Vivian's face. "I don't understand."

After another even longer pause, she said in a voice totally unlike her own, "So it's ... Yes, I see ... No." Vivian's hand shook. "When can I go take a look?"

I mouthed, "Take a look at what?"

As Vivian turned away from me, I noticed how white her face had become. She nodded and then said, "Yes. Daylight. I understand."

She hung up and just sat there, staring out at the road. I don't believe she saw anything at all.

"Vivian?"

She didn't answer.

"Vivian, what happened? Are you okay?"

Slow tears rolled down her cheeks. "My house is gone."

Chapter 9

Flash Flood

Dad, Vivian, and I went over to her house as soon as the sun rose. *House* was probably the wrong word to use because Vivian's yard was now just a debris-strewn mud pit. Her roof, cracked in two places, barely cleared the pile of mud. But otherwise, only bits and pieces of her house were still visible. The trees were half-buried too, as were Vivian's statues and yard.

"Maybe I should call Peter ..." Dad began.

But Vivian had drifted toward what was left of the house.

"It just needs to be cleaned up, right?" I said. "I mean, we can clean up all this dirt, and everything will be okay underneath. Right?"

"They haven't had a chance to check the house yet, Sadie. But I'm guessing it will be condemned. Houses aren't made to get wet and crack apart this way."

"But it's not wet anymore. I mean, they said the flood was so short ..."

"That's what a flash flood is," Dad said. "But there's structural damage, soggy drywall, and possibly mold left behind."

"But no one else's house was ..."

"There's a bit of flood damage downtown."

"A bit?"

"Nothing like this. Vivian's house sits lower than most, and she got the worst of it here, with the ice jam on that creek up behind her house, melting and dislodging all at once."

Vivian squatted down and dug into the dirt, coming up with something grubby cupped in her hands. I took a step closer but stopped when I saw the dead fish, his bright-red tail hanging at an awkward angle. All of her fish would be dead. All of her paintings would be destroyed. Her sculptures were broken and ruined. Anger rose, burning my throat. Why Vivian? Why not any other house? Why not ours?

Vivian started rocking back and forth. She hadn't said anything since she'd told me the house was gone. The last part of our drive home had terrified me, with the thick silence and her tears. She seemed trapped, frozen—as though a layer of ice had grown around her. Now, her quietness didn't feel comfortable, it was heavy—like Mom's silence when the sickness came. I knelt down and reached for her shoulder, but I couldn't bring myself to actually touch her.

Helplessness tore at me, ripping my insides and growing into thick black anger that demanded to be unleashed on someone, something, anything. Words, sense, nothing would come—just fury.

I clenched my fists, doing everything I could to hold myself together as Dad put his hand under Vivian's elbow and practically lifted her to her feet. "You'll come stay with us, of course."

She shook her head. Still, I managed to hold the monster inside.

"Yes," Dad said in a tone I knew meant business.

Breathe, Sadie. Breathe.

Vivian's voice cracked as she spoke. "I'll stay in an apartment over in Hiawatha. Could you drive me over there? I suppose I'll have to pick up my truck later."

"Vivian, no one expects ..." Dad began.

"I need my own space, Matthew. I need ..."

From where I stood behind her, I couldn't see her expression as she looked up at Dad. I saw his face harden, though, and then melt and settle into the look he sometimes gave Mom when there was nothing else he could do, other than help her to bed.

I wrestled my anger all the way to Hiawatha, hugging my arms around my body. If I let go, I might crack apart. Why was I so furious with Vivian? It didn't make sense. I wanted to shake her, to force her to speak. I wanted her to yell and cry so I didn't have to. I wanted to shout at Dad who hadn't fixed anything. Mostly, I wanted to scream at God, "It's not fair!"

I hated my hands, which fluttered around as though they could help if they could just find the right thing to do. All the things I wanted to say, like, "Don't move to Hiawatha, Vivian," and "I need you," were so selfish. I knew they were selfish. Still, I couldn't help thinking them.

We sat with Vivian while she signed a one-month lease and agreed to leave the walls in the apartment boring paper-white. Then Dad carried her suitcase upstairs. No bed, no couch, no TV. And definitely no colorful fishtank or art on the walls. No aprons or baking sheets or peanut butter cookie ingredients either.

She didn't seem to notice. She drifted from room to room and stared out each window.

"Vivian, Sadie and I will run home to gather some things for you. A pillow, food, blankets, and the air mattress. I'll ask Helen to come back with us so we can bring you the truck."

Vivian nodded slightly, still staring out the window. "I'll be okay, Matthew. You don't have to worry."

"We want you to have whatever you need. Should I leave Sadie here with you?"

Did she sense my reluctance? Is that why she said she needed a few minutes alone?

I was desperate to get away, to stop seeing Vivian in pain. I knew she wanted to be alone, but somehow leaving her felt wrong. Why should she suffer alone? Why should she suffer at all? Why her house, which was full of irreplaceable things?

Dad hit the steering wheel with his palm after we got back into the Jeep. "Why?"

I'd seen Dad lose his temper maybe twice before. I didn't know what to say.

Silence settled over us on the way home. Dad's mouth pressed into a tight line, and I curled up in my seat, physically holding myself together. Just two days ago, I'd laughed so hard that I couldn't breathe. Now I wasn't sure I'd ever laugh again. How could the entire world flip on its head because of one broken ice jam?

I buried my nose in my knees and tried not to see the broken fish every time I blinked. Tears rolled down my cheeks in slow, silent lines. I didn't bother to wipe them away.

"Sades," Dad said.

I didn't answer. I couldn't.

Chapter 10

Blank Pages

Back at the house, Dad and I rummaged through the linen closet and drawers. I found a spare apron in the kitchen. But even in his upset state, Dad forbade me from giving away his Sugar and Spice and Everything Nice apron, which would have been the perfect way to get rid of the hideous thing once and for all.

I gathered extra art supplies, paints, brushes, pencils, and a blank sketchbook I'd been saving for when I finished my current one. Fury ripped through me again as I turned through the blank pages. Not only had Vivian lost her house, but all she had now were blank pages. No old sketchbooks to flip through, no half-finished sketches to spark new ideas. Nothing. No art supplies in the world could fix that.

We packed towels, dishes, a cookie tray, sheets, blankets, a pillow, and our air mattress.

"This is a start." Dad looked over the pile. "Helen and Andrew have been collecting stuff too. Let's pick them up and then we can stop at the store. We'll pick up some food and dish soap and whatever else we can think of."

I nodded, still unable to speak, and helped carry the pile out to the Jeep.

A few bears rambled around the research station's yard when we arrived, and a girl I didn't know busily filled feeder boxes. With everything that had happened, I'd totally forgotten. Annabelle. Her blonde hair curled under at her shoulders, and she'd twisted and pinned a few strands here and there. White threads from her cutoff jeans hung against her perfectly tanned legs, and when she turned to look at the Jeep, my breath caught. Stunning green eyes, a perfect nose, and freckles scattered across her cheeks. She might be the prettiest girl I'd ever seen. She smiled at us as Andrew and Helen came out of the research station. Andrew walked over to Annabelle, put his hand on her shoulder, and told her something, his head close to her ear as he spoke.

Annabelle laughed and waved him away as he jogged over to the Jeep.

"Annabelle will stay and make sure everything's okay at the station," he told his mom. "She promised to call if the creek gets any higher."

"Hopefully Big Murphy will show up today or tomorrow. Annabelle knows to try to get him onto the scale if she sees him, right?"

"Yep. You know how she is with the bears."

Helen climbed into the Jeep. "My research assistant in training."

Andrew hesitated before getting in back with me. "Do you want to meet Annabelle now, Sadie?"

I shook my head. No need to explain that I'd rather do just about anything than meet Annabelle.

"Okay. How is Vivian doing?"

I shook my head again. The lump in my throat wouldn't allow me to speak, and I didn't know if it was because of Vivian or Annabelle.

"How's the health spa? Is Cindy settling in?" Helen asked Dad.

I stopped breathing. In all the commotion, I hadn't asked him about Mom. Dad didn't melt into a happy smile, but his shoulders didn't tighten in frustration either.

"The doctors are hopeful, but no significant results yet," Dad said, his tone guarded.

"What does that mean: 'hopeful'?" Andrew asked.

Leave it to Andrew to call Dad on the diplomacy.

"Hopeful that she can get back to a normal life."

Normal seemed impossible to me right now.

Andrew reached over and squeezed my hand. "I heard you were with Vivian when they called her about the flood. I'm sorry, Sades."

As soon as I could, I pulled my hand away and wrapped my arms around my knees again.

Andrew folded his arms and settled back into his seat. "We packed some things too. Kitchen stuff and a few books."

"So, who's Annabelle?" Dad asked Helen. "You're grooming a new assistant?"

"Not really. Her family runs a boating resort during tourist season, so they come up in the spring and stay through the summer. Annabelle fell in love with the bears the first summer we moved out here, and now they stay with us every year while they open up their lake house. To tell the truth, I don't think I could keep Annabelle away."

"She's a dancer, though," Andrew said. "I don't think she'll end up being a scientist. Sadie, I have so much news: Annabelle's going to be the lead in the show! She's perfect for it because the main character has to be a dancer—a really good one."

I forced a smile.

Andrew nodded at my necklace. "Pretty."

My cheeks burned. He'd given me the necklace. So why did I feel totally exposed for wearing it?

Andrew frowned and took my hand again. "I know you're worried about Vivian. I'm sorry, Sades."

Yes. I should be upset because of Vivian. But all I could think about now was Annabelle's perfectly freckled nose.

"We've improvised our way through the play a bunch of times," Andrew went on. "Penny set the scenes in their locations, and we have a loose idea of the flow. You'll love the story."

He was probably trying to distract me from thinking about Vivian, but I was mostly noticing how the pressure of his hand against mine clashed with the way he said Annabelle's name.

"The play starts in a forest shack, so we're using the Thompson's front porch. A messenger visits and announces that the king has requested their daughter — word has reached him about how she sings like a bird and dances like gravity doesn't exist. But the messenger is a liar. He takes the girl to the forest, binds her feet up in a music box, and collects money as people watch her sing and dance. That's the big thing your set crew will need to make — a music box. Oh, and the messenger's cart. Something big enough to hold Annabelle. She's not that big, but you know what I mean." There was that smile again — that Annabelle smile.

He looked as though he expected a reply. "Are you okay, Sades?"

He still held my hand. I pulled my fingers free. "Maybe we should talk about this later."

I dropped my face into my hands and rubbed my temples like I had a headache. Mostly, I didn't want to look at his face, all lit up like that.

"Vivian was going to help you with the set pieces, wasn't she, Sadie?" Helen asked from the front. "Maybe we should recruit some other helpers now. She'll be busy prepping pieces for her art show. Especially now, since —"

"She probably won't even be able to do the show," I snapped.

The Jeep went quiet.

Dad shot me a warning glance in the rearview mirror, and I mumbled an apology. "I'm just ..."

"You're upset," Helen said. "I know. It's okay." She turned

up the radio, and I leaned my head back against the seat and closed my eyes.

I felt Andrew watching me and turned away so my shoulder blocked most of his view of my face. He wanted to spend time with Annabelle? Fine. He didn't get to hold my hand, too.

From: Sadie Douglas
To: Pippa Reynolds
Date: Wednesday, April 11, 6:55.PM
Subject: Bad, bad, bad

Vivian's house flooded last night. All her art is gone. And it feels like she's gone too. She moved to Hiawatha this afternoon, which is only 25 minutes away, and Dad promised to take me out there for art lessons still ... but it doesn't feel the same. I saw Annabelle for the first time today. She's gorgeous. Uuugh!

Frankie emailed me her first drawing for the scavenger hunt yesterday. I need to reply to her, but I can't tell her about Vivian yet. Frankie already has too much to worry about. What should I do?

From: Sadie Douglas
To: Frankie Paulson
Date: Wednesday, April 11, 7:04 PM
Subject: Re: Old Woman

How long did it take you to find that old woman? I thought the same thing you did. In the first picture, when you were behind her, she looked so unhappy, stooped over on the stone steps. But then when you showed her face, her shoulders curled over to protect that kitten, and her eyes crinkled in a smile, I loved being wrong.

I'm sorry it took awhile for me to get back to you. Coming home was harder than I expected. I've attached my two-angle drawing for you — trees from the drive home. So you're opening an envelope every other day, right? I kept a copy of the list of tasks, so I'll keep my eyes open.

Chapter 11

Mom

The phone rang after I'd fallen asleep, and Dad picked it up on the first ring. I checked the clock: Eleven ten. Higgins jumped onto the bed and snuggled close, but I couldn't get comfortable. No call in the middle of the night can be good. After a few minutes, Dad's bedroom door opened, and his footsteps sounded on the stairs. Now I really had to know. I pulled on my slippers and hurried after him, Higgins on my heels. He was probably hoping for a treat.

Dad already had the frying pan out on the stove and was cracking an egg into a glass bowl. "Oh, Sades. I didn't mean to wake you."

"Who called?"

"Midnight snack?"

When I nodded, Dad cracked a few extra eggs into the bowl and added cheese and milk and spices. I sat at the table while Higgins lay on my feet, letting out a huge dog sigh.

"All right, Higgy." I took a treat from the jar and made him sit before giving it to him.

"So who was it?" I asked, sitting back down.

"Dr. Jenkins at the spa. Mom is having a difficult time with the detox treatment. Her heart isn't reacting well."

"Her heart? As in she had a heart attack?"

The eggs sizzled as Dad poured them into the pan. "No. Nothing so serious. Just arrhythmia. She's always had a little irregularity in her heart, but the treatment is making it act up."

"So she's getting worse."

Dad turned to look at me. "They'll take her off the treatment for a few days while her heart stabilizes, and then they'll try it again."

"And she'll have to stay there longer."

"Yes. But I know she wants to be home with us." Dad pushed the eggs around the pan with a spatula.

I kicked at the table leg, thinking about Mom in her hospital room all alone.

"What if . . . ?" I couldn't bring myself to finish the question.

"She'll be okay, Sadie. She can live with the disease. I probably shouldn't have suggested that she try the spa. I shouldn't have raised all of our hopes. Maybe we should just work on accepting the situation."

I kicked again — this time so hard that my foot rammed into the post. While I rubbed my big toe to stop the throbbing, Dad spooned eggs onto two plates and brought them over to the table.

I stabbed my fork into the pile. The eggs tasted like sandpaper, even though I'm sure they were just as good as Dad's eggs always were. Anger had taken over every part of my body — my nose, my mouth, my entire insides. My anger was so big that my skin couldn't hold it in. It burst out from every pore. My entire body burned with it.

"Sades, are you okay? You look flushed."

"I don't feel well."

Dad held his hand to my forehead. "You might have a fever. Maybe you should go back to bed."

I shivered. "Okay."

I felt hot, then cold, and then hot again. And my eyes stung. Higgins followed me upstairs, and I snuggled under the covers, not sure whether I should pull them up or throw them off. If only I could stay one temperature for a minute or two, then maybe I could decide.

Accepting the situation. Dad's words tumbled around in my head. How was I supposed to accept the fact that Mom would never be well? Never. As in never, ever? How could a person be fine one day, and then the very next day be sick with something that would last the rest of her life? For every holiday, every birthday, my graduation. Maybe even my wedding day (if I ever had one).

Thoughts of weddings made me think of Andrew and Annabelle, and now I did toss my covers off. I lay back, letting the cool night air hiss against my skin. Andrew's necklace burned against my neck. I flung it onto the bedside table and lay back, willing my mind to stop spinning. I wouldn't wear it anymore. Not ever.

I needed to pray. But what would I say? *God, help me accept the fact that Mom will be sick forever and that Andrew loves Annabelle? Help me accept that Vivian's house is gone and she has to start all over with her artwork?* I didn't want to accept any of those things. I closed my eyes and breathed until my heart slowed enough for me to fall into a toss-and-turn sleep.

I woke up a little later with my skin still on fire and my sheets a messy tangle. Tomorrow, I was supposed to go to the Tree House and spend the day working on set plans. Penny had scheduled the performance for one month from now, so the set pieces couldn't wait forever. We needed a music box and a cart, but I didn't know any of the other particulars. I shouldn't have cut Andrew off this afternoon. I just couldn't stand listening to him gush about Annabelle and how wonderful she was.

I rearranged my covers and opened my sketchbook, deliberately flipping past all of my prayer-pictures. From now on, I'd use the book to sketch set pieces. Business only. If God wanted to destroy Vivian's house — or allow her house to be destroyed — then I didn't feel like asking him for anything else. Talking to God seemed to lead to disasters, one way or the other. And I'd had more than my fair share of disasters. So much for God not giving me more than I could handle.

I tried not to picture Annabelle as I drew designs for the music box. It was supposed to be ornate and look like something that belonged to a king. So I'd need to find gold or silver paint. I'd pair whichever I found with deep red. Or maybe green. Apparently the messenger was poisoning the girl with lies, so maybe poison green would be appropriate.

Drawing only stirred up all of my frustrations, so I got out of bed and turned on my computer. Maybe Pips had answered my email.

From: Sadie Douglas
To: Pippa Reynolds
Date: Thursday, April 12, 1:55 AM
Subject: Re: Talk to him!!

I know. You're probably right, Pips. I just don't know how to ask him about Annabelle without sounding dumb. But I promise I'll try to talk to him tomorrow. Today, actually. I should be in bed, I know.

Thank you ...

P.S. I'm sorry that Alice is acting weird about you going to church. I guess she just misses you when the soccer team practices or plays on Sunday mornings? She'll get used to it eventually. We all know Alice doesn't like it when things change. And she doesn't like to feel left out either. Could you invite her to go to church with you sometime?

From: Sadie Douglas
To: Frankie Paulson
Date: Thursday, April 12, 2:01 AM
Subject: Re: Harder how?

I promise to tell you everything soon, Frankie. Maybe I'll call you later today. Don't ask why I'm up now. Long story.

Chapter 12

Annabelle

Inside the ring of girls, Annabelle leapt and spun, her hair golden in the sunlight against the green background of trees and forest. She whirled to a stop, laughing, and held her hands to her head.

"Makes you dizzy." She grinned at the girls' doubtful expressions around her. "But I promise you can all do it."

Everyone was mesmerized. I was mesmerized. I'd woken up feeling low but not sick anymore. And since I'd promised Pips I'd try talking to Andrew, I'd convinced Dad I felt well enough for rehearsal. So far, I'd holed up in my set-design station—a tarp and a picnic table near the Tree House—painting wooden crates to make them look old-fashioned. Penny promised that after rehearsal she'd talk me through other set pieces we'd need. For now, these crates would give actors places to sit while they watched Annabelle sing and dance. As far as I could tell, the play might as well be called "The Annabelle Show." She'd taken over everything, and she'd been here only a few days.

Brown paint dripped off my brush as I watched Annabelle, totally caught up in her smile. She radiated light, beautiful in a way I couldn't begin to describe. Partially it was the way she looked, but it was something deeper too. I wanted to watch her forever, study her until I learned how I could be beautiful like that.

And then I looked over at Andrew. He smiled that quiet smile, the Annabelle smile—a smile with all sorts of stories behind it. He'd known her for years. No one could say she was like a sister to him—not if they had eyes.

Annabelle slowed down the steps of the dance, showing them one at a time as the other girls followed her movements. Ruth was one of the dancers, her feet and arms gracefully bending and curving to mirror Annabelle's movements. I turned away. The other girls' movements were still jerky and clumsy, but Ruth seemed to melt under Annabelle's spell. My best friend and Andrew. Gone. Or nearly gone.

Focus on the painting, Sadie. That's your job.

As I finished one crate and reached for another, a hand touched my shoulder. I blinked a few times before turning, not wanting whoever it was to see me brush tears away. Pain burned in my chest, making it hard to breathe.

When I finally did turn, Ruth looked concerned. "Sadie, what's wrong?"

When I shook my head, she frowned. "We're all upset

about Viv, Sadie. But she doesn't expect us to sit around moping. Take a break and learn this dance. It's fun, I promise."

Moping. As though I could change the way I felt, just pull myself together. If I spoke, I knew my words would come out in embarrassing sobs, and I didn't want to cry in front of Ruth—not when she was in this good of a mood, glowing and totally caught up in the Annabelle trance. But I needed to ask someone about Annabelle and Andrew. Ruth should be the easy choice.

She leaned in close. "On my way over here, Cameron stopped me. Do you know what he said?"

I shook my head.

"He said my dancing was beautiful. He said it quiet and a little shy, like he really meant it. *Beautiful*, Sadie. He's never said anything like that to me before." She glanced over toward Andrew who was now laughing with Annabelle as she showed him a leaping turn and he tried to mimic her. "Come meet Annabelle. She's been talking about meeting you all day."

I dipped my brush into the paint and went back to my work.

"You can paint later, Sadie." Ruth tugged on my arm.

I bit down on my tongue to keep the tears from spilling over.

"What's wrong, Sadie?"

The tears spilled over anyway. I ran—not caring that paint dripped off my paintbrush—all the way to the sanctuary and into the bathroom. I locked the stall door, put down the toilet lid, and sat on top of it, wrapping my arms around my knees. Paint dripped through my fingers and onto the floor. I wouldn't have cared except the paint drips would be a total giveaway, and I didn't want anyone to find me. I set the paintbrush on the toilet tank and buried my face in my knees to muffle my sobs.

Annabelle. Annabelle. Her name pounded in my head, and her laughing face swum in front of my eyes. The horrible feeling burned in my chest, choking me, making me feel like I'd burn up from the inside. Later, they'd come into the bathroom and find a pile of ashes, all that was left of me.

A fresh wave of tears boiled out, a storm of feeling I couldn't sort through. After watching Annabelle for two seconds, seeing the way laughter bubbled up out of her and how she patiently reviewed a dance step with one of the younger girls, I knew she wasn't mean. And that made everything worse. She was just better than me. Better at dancing, sure, but better at being happy, too. Everyone wanted to be close to her. They couldn't help themselves. I would never be anything like that.

My mouth opened on its own, a soundless sob, and I couldn't stop the waves of misery rolling out of me, racking my body, making me shake with the pain of them.

Suddenly, I was on my feet, my fists slamming into the metal stall door. "It's not fair. It's not fair. It's not fair!"

I didn't care who heard me now. I didn't care if they all laughed and talked behind my back, or if they all thought I was jealous of Annabelle, or whatever. The problem was inside of me—deep inside—and I couldn't get it out. Mom. Vivian's house. Annabelle. Frankie was right: Why should we believe things will get better? Real life proves the opposite is true. Just when things seemed to be finally working, disaster struck. If I'd learned anything this year, you'd think I would have learned to expect disaster.

"Sadie?" Penny's voice echoed in the bathroom.

I caught my breath.

So maybe I *did* care if someone heard me. I didn't want to talk, but I knew Penny wouldn't let me off the hook.

"Sadie, I know you're in there. Open up."

I rubbed my eyes with my sleeve, and sticky paint smeared across my face. Still, I'd rather have paint streaks than tears. I opened the stall door, but I didn't step out.

"Any chance you want to talk in my office?" Penny asked. "I can lock the door so no one comes in."

Come to think of it, Penny's office was a better option than having someone walk in on us here. I followed her down the hall.

Chapter 13

Thunderclouds

As promised, Penny locked the door and then she handed me a super-sized box of tissues. I hesitated before sitting. No one wanted brown paint on their office furniture.

"It's okay. That's water-based paint. I'm not worried about it," Penny said.

I collapsed into a chair and held the tissue box close, glad for something to do with my hands. Penny sat on the desk with her feet up on the chair.

"This isn't just about Vivian, is it?" Penny asked.

I shook my head. I couldn't tell her it was about Annabelle. Even without talking to the girl, I was totally unhinged over her.

Penny rested her elbows on her knees. "How's your mom doing at the spa?"

Another touchy spot, but not the one that hurt most

right now. A fresh wave of guilt washed over me. I was more upset over Andrew than I was over Mom practically having a heart attack last night. What kind of crazy person was I?

I shrugged.

"You know, you're right. Life isn't fair. Sometimes the unfairness grows so big, it feels like we're drowning in it."

Penny was trying to help; I knew that. But she couldn't understand how my particular kind of drowning felt. It was selfish and rotten because all I wanted was for Annabelle to go away, to stop messing up my life and stealing all my friends.

"So, I promised to tell you more about the play." Though it seemed like a change of subject, Penny twisted and untwisted her fingers, like she was about to tell me about something important, something relevant.

"I wrote that story a long time ago, back when I was sixteen and away at summer camp. That year was full of disappointment. I'd trained as a gymnast, but at the meet where I tried to qualify for the Olympic team, I fell and shattered my leg in twelve places. Poof. Olympic hopes gone. Then while I was still in my cast, I came down with mono. So I was super sick, miserable, and ready to jump out of my skin with frustration. On top of all that, the boy I liked gave up on me because I was such a mess."

This wasn't making me feel any better. She was only proving my point: you couldn't count on anything or anyone — not even yourself. In the end, everything always fell apart.

Penny continued her story, "Then just before summer began, my grandma had a heart attack and moved into an assisted living facility. I'd been living with my grandma, so I had to move. My only other relative was an aunt, who ran a Christian summer camp up here, so to camp I went. I hated everything about it. All the campers seemed so sure that God was on their side, helping them; I couldn't stand all of their sureness. Not when I felt so confused.

"Early one morning, I had to get away. I ignored the distant rumbles of thunder and headed out to the woods on my crutches. I was deep in the forest when the rain started to fall. Then lightning cracked open the sky. I was trapped, alone, and terrified. I found a dry space underneath an over-hanging rock, and I curled up to wait out the storm. While I laid there, the storm battering all around me, this story arrived fully formed in my mind — as if someone whispered it into my ear."

Penny stopped twisting her fingers. "Can I show it to you?"

The dead quiet after her question caused me to look up. I could see in her face that she hadn't shown the story to anyone else.

"I told the others the cleaned-up version of the story. It's still a good story, but I think you might like to see the version I wrote as soon as I got out of that forest." She took a water-stained journal off her shelf and handed it to me. "Keep it for as long as you need to."

I set aside the tissues and took the book. "I don't think..."

"I'm not trying to convince you that life is fair. We both know it isn't fair most of the time. All I'm saying is that even when we can't see how, God takes the hard things in our lives and turns them into something beautiful."

An echo of what I'd said to Frankie. I realized I had the same argument she'd had.

"I don't want to believe in a God who ruins people's lives."

"Me neither," Penny said. "But bad things happen, regardless of what God desires. I want to believe he creates hope afterward."

I must have looked skeptical because Penny added, "You don't have to take my word for it, though. Just promise me you'll pay attention and stay open, okay? Miracles can't come into our lives if we shut them out."

I stared down at the notebook. Could an old story that Penny had written a long time ago help me? I had no idea how, but I wanted to believe it could. Right now, I needed some fresh air. I needed space. I needed to draw.

On my way outside, Andrew caught my arm. "Hold up, Sades."

Since Penny had been with me, I should have realized that rehearsal was now over. Of all people, why did Andrew have to be the one to stop me?

"Why didn't you learn the dance with the other girls?" he asked. "Annabelle said she hasn't met you yet."

"I was working on the crates." Right, genius; he could see that for himself.

Andrew's face creased in an unasked question. "Sadie ...?"

I stepped back. Being here with Andrew was too much. I'd start crying again, and then I'd be furious with myself, and everything would be worse.

"You're not wearing your necklace," he said, and then looked like he wished he hadn't.

I stared at my feet, willing him to go away. Promise or no promise, I couldn't ask him about Annabelle. Not when I felt like this.

"Look," Andrew said, "Mom asked me to invite you and your dad over for dinner on Sunday. She wants you to meet Annabelle's family, and she figures your house is kinda empty right now. Will you come?"

"You've already got guests." Another genius comment. Had someone switched off my brain?

Andrew hooked his thumbs in his back pockets, starting to look uncomfortable. "Are you upset about something?"

It took all my will power not to sigh.

Andrew must have seen the look cross my face. "I mean, I know there's a lot going on right now, with Vivian's house, and Frankie moving, and your mom ..."

And apparently, he'd fallen for Annabelle in the meantime. Or maybe Annabelle was always his girlfriend when she came to town. Maybe I was the winter substitute because she wasn't here. I went back to staring at my feet.

"Annabelle really wants you to come over," Andrew tried again after a long silence. "I've told her all about you."

Now I looked him straight in the eyes. "Really? There must have been excellent conversations."

Andrew winced as if I'd slapped him. "What are you talking about?"

"Nothing." I turned to go. I couldn't bring myself to ask: *So how long have you and Annabelle been a thing?*

Andrew caught my shoulder and pulled me around to look at him. "Sadie, if you're mad at me, just tell me. Tell me what I did, and we can work it out."

Images from this past year—skipping rocks, feeding the bears, drinking hot cocoa in the woods—flashed through my mind. I hadn't been pretending he liked me, right? Why was he so confused by my reaction?

"Maybe we should start with what you didn't do," I said.

Anger stormed across his face as he folded his arms. "Just tell me what's going on, Sadie."

"Yeah. Get mad at me, even though I didn't do anything. You're the one who suddenly has a girlfriend you never bothered to mention to me before."

His eyes hardened. "That's what you think? Really? That's what this is all about?"

My turn to fold my arms. No way he was throwing this back on me. Maybe I'd made up his feelings for me because I wanted so badly for him to like me. But I had no doubt about his feelings for Annabelle.

Dad honked the horn from the parking lot, and relief flooded through me. No more of this terrible conversation.

"I'll see you around, Andrew."

He stayed close on my heels as I headed out to the Jeep, and then he knocked on my window so I had to roll it down. "Mr. Douglas, my mom asked me to invite you both to dinner Sunday night."

"Wonderful," Dad beamed at Andrew. "We'd love to come."

As though I wasn't even there, Andrew and Dad talked over me for a bit until Andrew finally stepped back from the window. "See you tomorrow."

"Is Andrew okay?" Dad asked as we pulled away. "He looks worried."

"Sure, he's fine."

Dad looked closer at me. "And you, Sades? How are you doing?"

I sighed. "Can't I just be upset for once? Mom is sicker than ever, Vivian's house is a mess, and I just don't feel happy. Okay?"

Dad reached over and squeezed my hand. "Okay, Sades."

I turned up the radio, leaned back against my seat, and closed my eyes. Maybe I could get sick again. Or maybe I could come up with some other brilliant excuse, but somehow I had to get out of this dinner.

Chapter 14

Wild Encounter

I stayed in bed until late the next morning, avoiding the world.

Dad knocked and called through the bedroom door. "Going to rehearsal today, Sadie?"

"No," I mumbled into the pillows.

"Call if you need anything, then. I need to go to the DNR, and tonight I'll bring home chow mein. Sound good?"

"Okay." I waved him off.

Finally, I dragged myself to the phone to call Penny. I think she read between the lines when I said I wanted to stay home to work on my sketches. I just wasn't up for more Annabelle drama today. I tried to convince myself I was staying home for Frankie, which was partly true. No matter what was going on with Annabelle, with Vivian's house, with Mom, I couldn't ignore the scavenger hunt. Not when

Frankie was counting on me. I couldn't call her yet, not feeling like this. But I could look for the next object: Find and draw an object that catches your eye because it's an unusual color.

The only colorful things I could think of were fish. But Vivian's fish weren't unusually colored, and a picture of a broken fish would be the worst possible way to tell Frankie about the flash flood. I threw on jeans and a T-shirt, gathered my sketchbook and pencils, and as an afterthought slid Penny's journal into my backpack too. Vivian and I had designed the scavenger hunt while thinking about New York. So I hadn't planned what to draw here in Owl Creek. For one thing, I hadn't wanted to give myself an unfair advantage. But now I couldn't think of even one thing that was an unusual color. No lime green cars or pink hair in Owl Creek. Well, there was Penny's hair, but she didn't count. Everyone expected her hair to be some odd color or other.

"What do you say, Hig? Think we can find something unusually colored in the forest?"

Higgins' ears perked up at the word *forest*. He loved to chase squirrels and sniff and mark everything. I'd stopped leashing him during our walks in the woods because he practically pulled my arm out of the socket when he charged off into the wild. And anyway, he always came back. Bears stayed far away from us since Higgins hadn't learned the art of stealth, so I wasn't worried about having a wild encounter today.

I grabbed my coat and a few treats, and slung my backpack over my shoulder.

The morning was cold and still, as though the sky, the trees, and even the birds were all holding their breath, waiting for something. Higgins broke through the quiet like a motorboat cuts through glassy water, ruffling the bushes and filling the air with joyful barks. He'd be a terrible hunter, and I liked him that way.

Now that it was spring, Dad had applied for a new hunting license, and he'd started asking around for hunting buddies. He wanted to fit in with the hunters, to bridge the gap so he wouldn't seem so one-sided in his views about the bears. But everyone knew he wouldn't shoot a bear, so I didn't see what difference it made. Anyway, I was pretty sure we'd be moving soon. His job was just follow-up paperwork now. All of the community meetings were finished, and the decisions had been made. I hadn't expected to love Owl Creek and its residents so much. When we moved back to California, I'd miss Andrew and Ruth. But who knew if they'd miss me? They'd be hanging out with Annabelle. Perfect Annabelle.

I kicked a rock and it bounced right past Higgins. He tilted his head at me with droopy ears and tail.

"Sorry, Hig." I knelt down and scratched his ears.

Dampness from the mossy forest floor soaked into the knee of my jeans.

"I don't see anything unusually colored. Just regular bushes and flowers and trees."

Down here, the forest looked different. Flowers of every color bloomed: yellow, white, pink, even blue; but still, none qualified as unusually colored.

Off to my left, something crashed through the bushes, a large animal moving fast. I wasn't afraid of the bears, but I didn't want to be overrun by one—particularly not with Higgins here. I grabbed his collar and stayed as still as I could without letting go. I had seen mama bears with their cubs, and even though lots of people said they'd act protective, I'd learned that like all black bears, mama bears avoided confrontation. The most aggressive action I'd ever seen was when Patch had huffed at Andrew and stomped her front paws, blustering, so he would back away from her cub. But Higgins wasn't a human, so I couldn't explain bluster to him. Who knew what he would do if a bear huffed and stomped at him?

And then I saw them. July, followed by two cubs, one a deep black, and one pure white. My breath caught in my throat and I froze. A spirit bear. Helen said she'd never seen one in the wild. Last I'd heard, no one had seen July and her cubs yet this season, so they must have just come out of their den. We must have been upwind of the bears, because as they passed July and her cubs didn't notice us.

Even Higgy seemed to realize this bear was special. He sat at attention, ears pricked up, but didn't bark. Just as the bears were almost out of sight, the white one stopped and turned. For a long moment, I looked straight into its eyes, and it looked deep into mine. My heart raced and goose bumps shivered across my arms. This bear was more than just a bear. A sign ... the impossible standing right in front of me. After the cub followed July into the trees, I waited until I couldn't hear a sound before dropping to my knees to cradle Higgins' face in my hands.

"Did you see that, Hig?"

He stared back, his eyes deep and clear.

I looked around. We couldn't be the only two in the world who saw the bear cub pass by. But the forest was empty. Thunder rumbled overhead, reminding me of Penny's story in my backpack.

"Well, I found my unusually colored something," I told Higgins. "Now we'd better run."

I let go of his collar and we sprinted toward home. As I ran, I felt my story about the spirit cub mixing together with Penny's story about the summer storm. Higgins and I were drenched when we splashed into the yard. He shook the water off as we reached the porch, soaking me yet again before we went inside. I took my backpack to the bathroom, toweled off my hair, and sat on the edge of the tub, not wanting to wait another second to read Penny's journal. Somehow, I had to know what she'd written.

The story was strange and sad. The messenger Andrew had described was cruel. He forced the girl to dance and sing daily, telling her that one day she'd be good enough to perform for the king. Meanwhile, the girl tried and tried and tried, only to fall short every time. As hopelessness set in, the girl decided she'd never be good enough. She ran away from the messenger, away from her dream, and stumbled into a town where the local bakery shop owner took her in and gave her a job in his kitchen.

While she baked, she began to dance and sing once again — but for herself this time. She wasn't even thinking about performing publicly anymore. The townspeople would stop in the bakery to watch her. Yet the girl went about her work, refusing to perform for the customers. She believed she wasn't good enough to dance and sing for the king. And if she couldn't have her dream, then she didn't want to perform for anyone's enjoyment.

When the king showed up at the end of the story, he explained to the girl that he'd watched her dance and sing since she was a tiny child, and no amount of skill or ability made the slightest difference to him.

He'd been watching her from afar, no matter how lonely she'd felt, no matter how often she'd failed. He cared about her so much, he'd wanted her to learn to do what she loved in her own way, not to please him or anyone else.

Tears splashed onto the page as I read the story again. The words were scrawled and sometimes misspelled, as though they had tumbled out of Penny faster than she could think. Her story wasn't perfect or smooth, but I could feel her there in every sentence. The same way I could feel myself in one of my drawings. I could see why she'd wanted me to read the story from her journal, to feel the speed at which her hand had scrawled the words across the page. A rush of energy, like when you're lost and panicking and you finally see the way out. Or you at least have hope that you'll find a way out, like the way I'd felt just now when I saw the spirit cub.

I took Penny's journal back to my room and sat in the

window seat. Higgins jumped onto my lap and curled up. As I watched the trees and scratched Higgins's ears, I wondered what, exactly, I should do now. I felt ... different. Ideas floated into my mind—slowly, disjointed, forming a vague plan. I'd draw the cub for Frankie and email it to her. I'd try to stop lashing out at everyone. Maybe tomorrow I'd go see Vivian.

"What do you say, Hig?" As I spoke, he looked up at me, ears cocked. "Time to draw?"

He jumped off the seat, tail wagging.

"Okay. Maybe a treat first."

As I followed Higgins downstairs, I planned my drawing and tried to block out the lingering worry about Annabelle, Andrew, and Sunday's dinner.

From: Sadie Douglas
To: Pippa Reynolds
Date: Friday, April 13, 6:22 PM
Subject: RE: Talk yet?

Yes. Sorry I didn't email last night. I did try to avoid him, you were right. But he caught up with me before I left rehearsal. I tried to ask him about Annabelle, and he said, "That's what you think?" What does that mean? Why didn't he answer the question? And he invited Dad and me to dinner on Sunday with his mom and Annabelle's family. I didn't go to rehearsal today. So Alice didn't take it very well when you invited her to church, huh? I didn't realize she had such strong feelings about religion, or church. I wish I could help.

From: Sadie Douglas
To: Frankie Paulson
Date: Friday, April 13, 7:45 PM
Subject: For real

You're going to think I made up this drawing. But I really did see a spirit bear today, one of July's cubs. For some reason, I think it's a female bear. But I don't know for sure. Seeing the bear was like watching a magical creature step out of the trees. Like something from a fairytale that you can't quite believe.

Thank you for your drawing. Of course Chase would have a lavender suit. Did he really wear it to the ballet? Did you like the ballet? Living in New York must be so fun. Do you start school next week?

Okay, so here's what I didn't tell you before. Vivian's house flooded. Maybe she already called your mom about this because she might not be able to make enough pieces for the gallery show since everything was ruined. At least she thinks all of her sculptures are gone. Dad and I are going to try to salvage some stuff next week.

Some other bad things are happening here, too. Turns out, Annabelle is really pretty, and I'm almost positive that Andrew likes her. And Mom isn't getting better, either.

I didn't want to tell you these things before because I didn't want you to worry. So please don't worry, okay?

Chapter 15

Waves

"So what do you think of my drawing studio?" Vivian gestured at her cloth-draped living room.

She had promised not to paint the walls, but no one said anything about hanging fabric. Still, the bright yellow, red, and aquamarine didn't cheer me up. They were sad echoes of what she used to have.

Vivian went to her canvas and picked up her still-wet paintbrush. "I've missed you, Sadie."

I watched as she rounded out the corners of a large red circle in the middle of her canvas. "How can you stand it—being out here all alone, not having your house, not having anything?"

"Being alone helped, to tell you the truth. I felt like a turtle that needed to hide in my shell while I got used to the idea of not having the house anymore." She rinsed her brush and dipped it into the black paint.

"But how can you get used to the idea of losing all of that art?"

She stopped and looked at me. "It wasn't the art that hurt, Sadie. I can make new art. The memories are what I can't bear to lose."

It was a punch to my stomach. Yes. Vivian and her husband had lived in that house for a long time before he died. Every room would have held memories. The way you can find a forgotten ornament from last Christmas and how the smell of cinnamon makes you feel like you're back in your pajamas opening presents around the tree.

"So you're just accepting that the house is gone?"

"The house is gone, Sadie, whether I accept it or not. Right now, I feel particularly angry about losing something bigger than a house. My life, I guess."

"You don't seem angry."

"Because I'm painting." Vivian removed a drop cloth from a nearby easel, revealing a red canvas with jagged black slashes across it.

The next drop cloth covered a completely black canvas with deep blue slashes. On they went, canvas after canvas, each with angles and colors that screamed, "Why? Why? Why?"

"This helps you?" I asked.

"If I didn't paint it out, I'd explode."

Explode was the perfect word. All the calm from yesterday — after seeing the cub and reading Penny's story — had evaporated the minute I'd walked into Vivian's apartment. Anger billowed like storm clouds inside of me, making me wonder if I might just explode. Right here. In Vivian's fabric-strewn living room. The locked box that I'd drawn at the bottom of the ocean floated into my mind as I looked at the blank canvas Vivian had set out for me. The mess inside the box rattled around, trying to get free, but I knew I couldn't handle any more than I had to deal with already.

You don't have to open it, not now. It's enough to know it's there.

The thought slipped into my mind like smoke seeping under a door, surprising me with its clarity. I hadn't been willing to draw or even talk to God these last few days. I hadn't considered that he might still be close by, watching, caring about what was going on. I'd convinced myself he didn't care, actually. Now, after seeing the spirit bear yesterday and having this thought arrive, uninvited, I wasn't so sure.

I realized I was staring, unseeing, at Vivian's canvas. "You always tell me to draw what I see. These are just lines and colors."

"These are the images I see in my head," Vivian said. "So instead of letting them jab me, I'm throwing them out onto the page."

"And then they're gone?"

"No. But when you can see something, it's much less intimidating than when you feel something you can't define." She handed me brushes and pointed to a canvas. "That one's yours. Make anything you like."

I hadn't worked with brushes and paint since second grade. Was I supposed to copy Vivian, just lay down a bright color and then start flinging paint around?

"This kind of painting isn't about planning or thinking, Sadie." Sometimes it was like Vivian could read my mind. "Just let yourself go."

I took a can of aqua paint over to the canvas. The deep-sea color stood out against my paintbrush's black bristles. Thinking of my locked box rattling around, I suddenly wanted to paint waves — crashing and foaming and tearing. My hand moved on its own, splashing paint in waves and swirls across the canvas. Over and over I dipped my brush, letting the strokes fill the canvas with color. They didn't look exactly like waves, but they moved around the page, up and over one another.

At the bottom of the canvas, I'd left a calm spot in the middle. I found a smaller brush and some black paint. Instead of drawing the box and key again, I formed the silhouette of a person kneeling with her hands over her head, trying to protect herself from the stormy sea. I stepped back. Foam. The waves needed white water. A brush wouldn't do it, so I used one of Vivian's paint sponges. I sponged white paint in foamy masses at the edges of the waves, working the paint until the white and blue smeared together in some places. When I finally stepped back to look, Vivian joined me.

"Yes," she said. "That's the kind of painting I'm talking about." She pointed to the stack of canvases. "Want to try another?"

Anyone else would have asked about the figure, about the waves, about what was going on with me. Vivian knew the last thing I needed to do right now was to talk. Instead, I needed to paint all of the things I couldn't see — all of the mess that foamed up inside of me — and figure out if I could find a way through it all.

I rinsed out my brush and set a new canvas on the easel. This time, I started with black and roughly outlined a girl on a swing, her legs extended. That day on the swings with Frankie, I'd wanted to draw the air around me, the way I'd felt in that moment — totally lost in happiness. With a set of brushes and multiple colors of bright paint, I shaped thick streaks of color in swirling strokes around the girl, trying to make the colors twist into one another the way wind moves in unpredictable fits and starts. I didn't want the colors to mix and become muddy, so I kept rinsing my brushes, using thick streaks of color instead of small amounts of paint. The texture of the paint, glossy on the canvas, gave the air that tangible feeling I'd wanted to show but hadn't been able to picture in my mind. Painting this way, not thinking first, gave me the same feeling as drawing in my journal. I missed that open, free feeling. I was listening instead of working hard.

Maybe I'd been too quick to stop drawing at night. To block out what had been so important to me. And blocking out God didn't seem to work anyway, since he slipped words into my mind when I least expected them.

I stepped back from my canvas, almost breathless from the speed at which I'd been painting.

Vivian stopped painting too and looked at me.

"I saw a spirit bear," I said.

Her eyes went wide. "In the forest?"

"One of July's cubs," I said. "It stopped and looked at me, as though it wanted to tell me something."

"The legend says they were meant to bring hope, new possibilities."

"I used it for my object of an unusual color. For Frankie."

Vivian smiled. "Perfect. She needs hopeful reminders."

She studied my latest painting. "You've got it. That's the swing from our drive to New York, isn't it?"

"Yes."

"Well." Vivian was smiling, the first real smile I'd seen from her since we found her house under a thick layer of mud. "I should have given you paint sooner. Looks like you've found your medium."

Yes. The image was more vivid than what I'd seen in my mind, unlike any of my drawings to this point. I'd only come close to drawing what I wanted, never gone past my hopes.

I grinned at Vivian. "Yeah. I could get used to paint."

"And cookies?" she asked.

"Definitely cookies." I followed her into the kitchen. As I went, the thought crystallized. Anger wasn't getting me anywhere. Vivian was better because she was doing something. I could do that too. I'd work on set pieces and help wherever I was needed. If I just kept pretending I was all right, then eventually I'd convince myself I actually was all right. The plan would work. It had to because I didn't think I could sit in the middle of this stormy sea for even a second longer without drowning.

From: Sadie Douglas
To: Pippa Reynolds
Date: Saturday, April 14, 7:12 PM
Subject: RE: Ballooning Birthday

Are you kidding me? You're going up in a hot air balloon with the girls for your birthday?? I so wish I was there. You have to take pictures. Wow!

I'm going to rehearsal tomorrow afternoon to work on sets. I saw Vivian today, and we painted. I LOVE paint, Pips.

I have to go to the Annabelle dinner tomorrow night. I've managed to avoid her until now. I'm trying to figure out what I'll say to her. If I have a lot to talk about, maybe we won't get into anything uncomfortable. I guess we can talk about bears and her dancing ... that's something, anyway.

Miss you ...

Chapter 16

Meaningless Words

You're late," Ruth called, bounding over to me as I walked toward the set-building area. We did this every once in a while, pushed our cheerfulness over the top to make each other smile. But her smile faded pretty quickly as she came close enough to see my face.

"Okay, Sadie. What's up? What happened the other day? I looked for you everywhere, but you were gone. Did I say something wrong?" Tiny frown lines furrowed between her eyebrows, such a contrast to how she'd looked just minutes before when she was talking to Annabelle.

Perfect. Annabelle made everyone smile and I made them frown. My throat closed up. Tears weren't very far behind. No. I'd decided to act normal until I felt normal, and I wasn't going to fall apart again. So I forced myself to ask the question, right that minute.

"Are Annabelle and Andrew . . . ?" When my voice cracked, I stopped speaking.

"Are they what?" Ruth asked, confusion clouding her face. Then suddenly, she burst out laughing, catching me totally by surprise. "Sadie!"

"What?"

With hands on hips now, her smile was a mixture of disbelief and amusement. "I thought you were upset about Vivian or your mom or something, but this is about Annabelle? Why didn't you just ask me?"

"I . . ." The words wouldn't come.

"Well, they're just friends, Sadie. I promise." Ruth glanced over at Annabelle, who was motioning for us to join her, Cameron, and Andrew.

"We all want—come on, let me introduce you." Ruth took my arm.

Penny hurried over from the office. I'd never been so happy to see her. I'd have to meet Annabelle tonight at dinner, but I wanted to do it my own way, on my own terms. I didn't want to meet her with Andrew, Ruth, and Cameron watching.

"Sadie, I found a volunteer to help you with the sets," Penny said when she reached us. "Annabelle's dad offered to cut the boards for all the big pieces."

I tossed a "Help me!" look at Ruth, who just smiled as if to say, "See? Even her dad is nice."

"I'd like to schedule him to come as soon as you're ready with drawings and dimensions. But you'll need to see the play first, so . . ."

The music started.

"That's my cue. Come over when you can — okay, Sadie?" Ruth squeezed my arm and left.

Penny looked closely at my face; I felt naked, exposed.

"I'm fine," I said before she could ask.

"Did you read my story?" she asked.

"Oh, I almost forgot." I pulled the water-stained journal from my bag. "Thank you. I really loved it."

The words felt too simple, too light to express what I meant to say.

But Penny winked and said, "I thought you might."

She took the journal and handed me a list. "You'll see how we smoothed out the rough parts when you watch the play. This list covers the set pieces we'll need. We can discuss them at the run-through on Tuesday. Can you come after school?"

"Sure." I'd decided to distract myself by working on set pieces, so I might as well start as soon as possible.

Until Dad came to pick me up, I pretended to be much busier than I actually was so I wouldn't have to watch the rehearsal. We hurried home so I'd have time to clean up and get ready for dinner.

As I finished braiding my hair, Dad called upstairs, "Sadie, come talk to Mom!"

I frowned at myself in the mirror. Mom, too? After not talking to her for so long, she was calling tonight?

"Sades," Dad poked his head in my door and held out the phone. "Mom's waiting."

Big breath. First, Mom. Then Andrew and Annabelle. I could do this. I took the phone and watched my face break into a too-big smile in the mirror.

"Mom! How are you feeling?"

Her voice was controlled as she answered, "I'm doing well, Sadie. Really well. They're putting me back on the treatment today."

I wanted to ask her about the heart episode. I wanted to ask her if she really thought the treatment was a good idea. But, like always, I said none of these things.

Instead, I pretended everything was all right. "I'm sure it will help you a lot."

"Dad told me about Vivian's house. I'm so sorry, Sadie." The line crackled.

I practiced my everything-is-fine tone. "Well, she's doing okay, and she may still be able to do a smaller show in New York."

"I wish I could be there for you, Sadie."

I nodded and then realized she wouldn't know that I'd nodded.

The silence stretched long, so I said, "I miss you, Mom."

Another long silence. She was probably rubbing the bridge of her nose the way she sometimes did when she had to give me bad news.

Finally, she said, "They're saying I might have to stay until the end of April, Sadie. I'm so sorry."

I'd heard it was through the end of May. Either they hadn't told her, or she thought easing me into the extended trip would be better.

"It's okay, Mom."

The conversation was so hollow, we might as well have been standing at the bottom of our own canyons, shouting meaningless words to each other that echoed from rock to rock. By the time we heard one another, our words had broken into sounds that made no sense.

Dad stood in the doorway watching me talk, his face hard to read.

"Um, Mom? Dad and I have to go now. We're going to have dinner with Helen and Andrew and this family who's staying with them."

"I heard there was a new girl in town. I hope she'll be another friend for you, especially now that Frankie is gone."

I stared my reflection down as I answered, "Yeah. Maybe. See you soon, Mom."

Even though I wanted to say "I love you," I couldn't do it. Not after such a lie-filled conversation. I'd save those words for a moment when I felt truthful.

"Bye, Sadie."

I hung up and handed the phone to Dad. "Ready to go?"

"Sadie ..." Dad's voice was full of questions that I didn't want to answer.

"They're waiting, right?" I walked past him into the hallway, down the stairs, and out to the Jeep.

I turned up the music during the ride over to Andrew's house, choosing a country station because I knew I could con Dad into singing along, too. He glanced at me and even cracked a smile, so I knew I was doing well. If I could convince Dad, I could convince anyone.

Chapter 17

Disaster for Dinner

Andrew watched me warily as I stepped into the cabin, probably expecting another blow-up. I ignored him and walked straight over to Annabelle. Dad and the other adults went outside to look at the bears.

"Hi," I said to Annabelle.

"Hi yourself." She gave me one of her dimpled smiles.

Up close she was, if possible, even more perfect. Straight, white teeth, and smooth skin frosted with freckles. Not even a single tiny zit. I forced myself to keep smiling.

"Your dance for the play looks really good."

"You think so?" she asked. "There might be too much spinning. I don't want anyone to trip and fall."

"Bea tripped and skinned her knee," Andrew said. "And Annabelle won't stop blaming herself."

Annabelle elbowed him. "And Andrew won't stop giving me a hard time. He treats me like I'm his little sister or something."

Or something. I needed an escape plan. "I'll go see if Helen needs help setting the table."

"I'll help." Annabelle followed me.

As I placed each napkin, she added a fork. "We thought maybe we could come over tomorrow and help you work at Vivian's house. You're going to do some clean up?"

I shrugged. "Dad tells me not to get my hopes up. But maybe we can salvage some of the larger sculptures from the yard."

"It's just the weight of the mud and the force of the flash flood." Andrew leaned against the counter as we finished with the utensils and started on the water glasses.

"Well, anyway, I'm going to try." As I filled the water pitcher, the adults came back in.

"Ah, it smells delicious," Annabelle's dad announced, much louder than necessary for the small space. "Doesn't it smell delicious, Annabelle?"

Annabelle gave her dad a forced smile that I didn't understand, while her mom kissed her on the cheek. "Thank you for helping, sweetheart."

They were like a family of superheroes. Annabelle's dad with his booming, I'm-here-to-save-the-world voice, and her mom with her designer jeans and silk tank top that showed off toned arms. She looked like a cop or a spy in the movies, both beautiful and deadly. And then Annabelle, of course, seemed to be best at everything, so far as I could tell.

"So this is the famous Sadie," Annabelle's dad said,

coming over to shake my hand. "I'm Jack Reid, and this is my wife, Leila."

Annabelle's mom clasped my hand between hers. "Nice to meet you, sweetheart."

I couldn't imagine calling them anything other than Mr. and Mrs. Reid.

Helen handed me the salad bowl to carry to the table, while she brought over the chicken casserole. "Looks like we're all set."

Annabelle sat between her mom and dad, across the table from Andrew, so I ended up sitting between Andrew and Dad. Perfect. Now we could admire her side by side.

"So, I hear I'm helping you build a music box for our Annabelle," Mr. Reid said to me as we passed the salad around the table.

"Yes." I hoped a short answer would deflect his attention to someone else.

"Seems difficult to build something big enough to hold a—"

Mrs. Reid interrupted him with a sharp look. "Not that Annabelle's big ..."

"No." Mr Reid laughed, "Our Annabelle is perfect. She knows that. Casserole?"

Annabelle stared at her hands while he spooned casserole onto her plate.

"Looks like we can open the lake house by next week." Mrs. Reid smiled brightly around the table. "You're all welcome to come visit or go boating anytime."

"Wildflowers are blooming on all the little islands, and it's a perfect time to go camping," Mr. Reid said. "We have tons of early campers this year, too. Lots of people who can see our Annabelle's show."

"It's not just my show, Dad." Annabelle looked over at Andrew before smiling at her dad, but her eyes were different than usual. Still bright, but a little too bright.

Andrew frowned at Annabelle's plate, which was still full of salad and casserole.

Mr. Reid took a big bite. "This casserole is delicious, Helen."

"And the veggies are so fresh," Mrs. Reid added.

Helen smiled. "Well, I slaved away in the kitchen."

It felt like they were having a conversation beyond what they were saying. I felt so out of it these days, I had no idea if I was just reading too much into things.

Dad might have felt the strange tension too because he changed the subject. "So Sadie told me that one of July's cubs is a spirit bear."

Helen and Andrew both spun in their chairs to look at me.

"There hasn't been a spirit bear in this area for as long as I've been here," Helen said. "Are you sure that's what you saw, Sadie?"

"She had two cubs with her, one black and one completely white." I stared down at my fork, wishing I could explain it better.

If Annabelle were describing a spirit bear, she'd probably gush and beam at everyone. But I couldn't do that. I couldn't even look up because tears filled my eyes.

"I'm sorry, Sadie," Helen said. "I didn't mean to pounce on you. I've been waiting to see July this season, and I'm astounded by this news. How incredible!"

"What's a spirit bear?" Mr Reid asked.

"The Canadian First Nations once believed that the all-white spirit bears, who look like ghosts, had mythical powers," Helen explained. "And they also believed the Creator made them white to remind them of the Ice Age and the troubles they no longer had to face. They're also known as the Kermode bear, and mostly found in British Columbia."

"What do you think, Sadie? Did the bear have special powers?" Annabelle asked.

Fortunately, my mouth was full. I don't know how I would have answered her if it hadn't been. Andrew jumped in, to my surprise.

"It was probably one of those experiences you can't really describe." He put his hand on my shoulder. "Must have been incredible."

I looked down quickly because once again, my eyes filled with tears. I was a mess. Helen seemed to notice my struggle because she quickly changed the subject. As the attention turned away from me, I took a deep breath and shoved my food around my plate. The evening was a failure and dinner was only half over. I'd almost cried twice, totally failing to prove how incredibly happy I was. I felt like Vivian's turtle but without its protective shell.

It would be a long night.

From: Sadie Douglas
To: Pippa Reynolds
Date: Sunday, April 15, 9:24 PM
Subject: Remember the Hamiltons?

Do you remember Serena? She lived with her mom and dad in that big house on the hill? Remember how perfect everything was in their house? Her walk-in closet organized by color? And the snacks her mom would send to school in a bento box, and each mini-bite looked like it had been created by a professional chef?

That's what Annabelle's family is like. Perfect. Uuuuuuughhhhh. Glad to hear things are better with Alice. Sorry that you feel like you can't talk about church with her, though. That must be weird, to have to avoid subjects with the girls. I mean, we never were like that. Just a few more days until your birthday!!!

From: Sadie Douglas
To: Frankie Paulson
Date: Sunday, April 15, 9:30 PM
Subject: Re: Left Behind

It's weird that you randomly met someone from your new school! Was she nice? Do you think you'll like it there?

I liked the drawing of the umbrella left behind on a park bench, and your story about someone deciding to walk home in the rain. I like that idea more than someone just forgetting her umbrella. I feel like the sky is crying too, sometimes, when it rains.

Are you okay?

I'll look for my abandoned object for the scavenger hunt tomorrow. I'm working over at Vivian's house because we don't have to go back to school until Tuesday. Monday is a teacher in-service day. The bad news is that Annabelle and Andrew are also coming to help clean up at Vivian's house. ☹

Chapter 18

Digging

My reflection stared back at me, my eyes determined. Yes. I *will* go to Vivian's house today. I will find an abandoned object for Frankie, and I won't obsess over Andrew and Annabelle. I dropped my forehead against the cold glass and groaned. Sometimes being a girl was lame.

"Sadie," Dad called from downstairs. "You ready to go?"

I lifted my head and stared myself down. "You can do this, Sadie."

"Sadie?"

"Coming!"

Higgins followed me downstairs, nosing my hand all the way. Even though Dad pointed out all the reasons we shouldn't bring Higgins to the cleanup, I promised to watch him and give him a bath afterward and be completely responsible. I needed someone to bury my face in when

Annabelle became too much. Higgins sat on my lap with his head hanging out the Jeep window, tongue and ears flapping, as we drove. I held my arms up to block the drool flying out of his mouth, but he kept turning to me and giving me a "What's your problem?" look, making me laugh too hard to shield myself.

"It's good to hear you laugh," Dad said. "I've been worried about you, Sades."

"I'm fine," I said, my automatic response.

"Well, if you weren't, I'd understand." Dad rubbed his hand across the steering wheel. "We both want Mom to come home, and I know the flood was a huge blow for you."

I shrugged. "I'm fine" slipped out pretty easily now, but a further explanation might break down the wall I'd carefully constructed. And that couldn't happen — not even with Dad. I needed that wall right now, especially now, on our way to see Annabelle.

"It's okay to feel upset, Sadie. To let people help you," Dad said, as though he'd read my mind.

Maybe. But how could anyone help me? Annabelle was here to stay, Andrew felt whatever he felt about her, the flood damage couldn't be undone, and Mom probably wasn't going to get any better — at least not the way I wanted her to. I could whine and complain all I wanted, but none of those facts would change.

Life just wasn't fair. I'd told Frankie that unfairness was an opportunity for something better; now I wasn't so sure. In fact, I was almost convinced I'd been flat-out wrong.

Maybe I should tell Frankie that tonight when I sent her whatever drawing I was supposed to send to her.

When I'd originally planned the hunt, I'd planned to send her hopeful pictures. Images to remind her that life isn't always disappointing. Now, though, I was pretty sure life was simply unfair and you had to deal. No silver lining.

"Penny for your thoughts?" Dad said.

I scratched Higgy's ear, trying to get a grip on my emotions. "Umm ... Viv's statues. Andrew thinks the force of the flood will have cracked them all. Do you think that's true?"

"That's highly likely. Vivian is almost sure they're all gone. But she loves to reuse things. So even if we can't salvage the statues, it's worth looking for any ceramic pieces we can save."

"She won't want to use them, will she?" I frowned. "They'd be reminders of what happened."

Dad pulled into Vivian's driveway. "It can't hurt to find what's here, no matter what."

I climbed out and went directly to the area where the statues were buried. No one was here yet, and I was glad Dad had pushed me to hurry. I looped Higgins's leash around a nearby tree and went back to the Jeep for the shovel.

"I'm going to start over by the house," Dad said. "You'll be all right on your own?"

"Yeah. Higgy's here to keep me company."

Fortunately, it hadn't rained for the past few days, so the dirt was relatively dry as I started digging. Farther down, though, it was still damp, and I was head-to-toe mud by the time Annabelle and Andrew arrived. Together, of course.

I pushed the shovel into the ground and wiped sweat off my forehead with my sleeve as they got out of Helen's car. I was most likely just smearing mud across my face. My almost-unburied statue looked good, though. No cracks to be seen. Maybe I could at least prove Andrew wrong.

Annabelle walked over to me while Andrew went to talk with Dad. "Wow, look at you! Is it broken?

I looked down at the mud-caked statue. "So far so good."

Annabelle crouched down to look closer. "What's that, though?"

I knelt down too. A ragged crack showed just above the dirt line. The mud held the statue together now, but soon, once I'd cleared it all away, the statue would topple.

"It's still worth unburying, though." Annabelle gave me a sympathetic smile. "She might be able to patch it, or use parts of it, or something."

A long-ago conversation with Vivian came back to me. She'd forced me to draw over my mistakes, no matter what happened, and make art out of the mess. The statue, coated with grime and cracked in at least one crucial place, was too much to salvage. It would be like trying to patch your heart together after it had been ripped in two. Suddenly, I couldn't bear this anymore. I didn't want to dig up statues. I understood why Vivian had simply walked away. Better to start over than deal with this kind of pain.

"Sadie?" Annabelle was saying. "Are you okay?"

I'd completely lost focus. Instead of showing my "Everything is fine" face to Annabelle, I was crumbling. Right here in front of her.

"I'm fine," I forced myself to say. The words left a bitter taste in my mouth, but I managed a smile. "Just a little muddy."

"Oh!" Annabelle beamed. "I brought towels and wet wipes and hand sanitizer. And some first-aid stuff too, just in case. I'll get you something to clean up with."

She ran over to the car. Every step she took, even when she wasn't trying, looked like a dance. She hurried back, her arms full of supplies, with Andrew in tow.

"So, it's broken, Sades?" Andrew looked genuinely disappointed. No I-told-you-so look at all. Still, he must be thinking it.

I shrugged. "You were right. No point in unburying these, really."

Annabelle handed me a wet wipe, and I used it to clean my face and hands.

"Your dad said she might be able to reuse the ceramic pieces." Andrew leaned close, testing the looseness of a yellow-glazed piece.

They might as well stick needles in me, or poke and prod me in all the places that hurt. All I wanted was to get away from them. I didn't want Vivian to salvage the pieces. I wanted her to have them back, whole and fixed. I couldn't imagine delivering one of these statues to her just so she could dig out the ceramic shards and use them in another piece. Vivian didn't pick and pry. She tossed dishes at the wall—wild and free—and all the energy and emotion went into her piece.

"We should let it go," I mumbled.

Andrew looked up from the statue. "What?"

"Just let it go," I said, louder now. "It's broken. She won't want it. I know she won't."

He reached out to touch my shoulder. "But Sades, you worked so—"

"I have to go." I untied Higgins and hurried out into the forest.

Higgins pulled at the end of his leash, so I unclipped him and let him take the lead. I didn't mind following. Not wanting to come back empty-handed, I looked for something to use for the next clue in the scavenger hunt:

Find something abandoned that makes you think of a story.

I scanned the forest floor for options. Leaves, flowers, mushrooms. Nothing abandoned. Higgins and I wandered through the underbrush until I almost gave up.

And then I saw it, tucked under a curling vine and half-buried in the dirt. I called Higgins, clipped the leash to his collar, and took out my sketchbook. I sketched quickly, capturing the chain and the curve of gold just as they were right now. Still, my fingers itched to pull it out and examine it. I finished sketching and jotted a line under my picture, "The prince dropped his pocket watch while trying to catch up with the girl who ran off into the forest, seeming to disappear ..."

If only Andrew would chase after me. But he wouldn't, not as long as he was busy with Annabelle.

I wriggled the watch out of the ground and brushed it off.

"What is this, Hig?" I asked.

He cocked his head, questioning.

The initials DH were etched into the gold cover. Vivian's husband's name had been David, and their last name was Harris. Could this have belonged to him? I ran my fingers over the initials.

Annabelle's laughter rang through the trees, and I closed my eyes. I'd found what I'd been looking for, and I'd drawn my sketch. Probably now, I should go back to the others.

Please help me.

I whispered the prayer before I stopped to think. Did I want to bring God into this? The watch seemed to warm in my hand. Was it just my imagination? Maybe not. I needed reminders that God is here, helping me, listening to me. Was it so impossible that he'd respond to my prayer this way? God had shown up in very tangible ways for me so far. Sometimes, I could almost feel him put his hand on my shoulder.

I curled my fingers tighter around the watch, drawing the warmth into my skin.

Stay with me. I need you.

Once the watch cooled, I slid it into my backpack along

with my sketchbook and pencils. I grabbed Higgins's leash and took a deep breath before heading back toward the others.

From: Sadie Douglas
To: Frankie Paulson
Date: Monday, April 16, 7:22 PM
Subject: DH

So I think the pocket watch I found (drawings attached) belonged to Vivian's husband. He was David Harris, right? What do you think? Should I show the watch to Vivian? She said the worst part of losing her house was losing her memories. And I know a watch isn't really a memory, but a house isn't either. It's an object that holds memories, right? So you'd think having the watch would be better than not having it. I don't know.

I hope you like the drawings. This scavenger hunt is turning out to be more interesting than I expected.

Chapter 19

A Real Promise

I don't know why I didn't expect it. Maybe because Andrew was homeschooled, I didn't expect Annabelle to show up at school. But here she was, sitting in Frankie's newly vacated desk.

Abby and Erin sat on the adjoining desks, talking and laughing with her as though school was a slumber party in disguise. Annabelle seemed to fit in better—in my town, my school, my life—than I did. I was once again the new girl, and she'd been here forever, even though she'd just shown up.

I dropped my backpack on the floor by my desk and slid into my seat just as Ruth came through the door. I resisted the urge to put my head on my desk. I was Sadie the Strong. Sadie the Happy. Sadie the Not Bothered by Annabelle Barging Into My Life and Taking Up All the Space So the Rest of Us Have to Shuffle Around the Edges.

As soon as Ruth saw Annabelle, her face lit up. She bounded halfway across the room before she even glanced my way.

She called out, "Hey, Sades! What are you doing over there?" and then she hurried off to join Abby, Erin, and Annabelle.

As though sitting at my own desk was strange. As though I, like everyone else, should stick like chewed-up gum to Annabelle's side.

Fortunately, Ms. Barton came through the door next. "Morning, class."

She looked toward the disturbance at Frankie's old desk. "Oh, good morning, Annabelle. I didn't expect you for a few more weeks."

Annabelle smiled. "Dad wanted to open the boathouse. We have lots of early bookings."

"Well, we're glad to have you." Ms. Barton set her books on her desk. "I see you found Frankie's desk. She's left us, so you're welcome to sit there for the remainder of the year."

As though Annabelle could slip into the space that Frankie had left behind. The trouble was, Annabelle made my life feel like a lie. I'd thought Ruth liked me more than anyone else in Owl Creek, with the exception of Cameron, of course. And I'd become too comfortable expecting special treatment from Andrew after our candlelit Christmas Eve and prank-filled Valentine's Day. Yet Annabelle changed all of that simply by showing up.

My hands shook as I took out my pencil and flipped to the right page in the math book. Ms. Barton explained how x related to y, but I couldn't focus. On a good day, I struggled to keep up in math. Today, I was fully lost. Still, I wrote numbers in long strings down my page, sticking to the plan. I'm busy. I'm fine. Everything is all right.

I volunteered for classroom cleanup during lunch period so I could avoid eating with Ruth and Annabelle, and I spent the day with my head down. I had to put up with Annabelle tonight at play rehearsal too, so I had to save up my patience.

I hung back as long as I could after the final bell rang, but Ruth was still in the hallway when I left the classroom.

"Hey, Sades." She crossed the hallway, her face serious.

"Hey." I mentally prepared my I'm-fine speech.

Ruth looked both ways down the hallway, but we were alone. "Look," she said. "You're upsetting Annabelle."

I wasn't sure I'd heard her right. "I'm what?"

"You're obviously avoiding her, and she thinks she did something wrong."

"Why does Annabelle care what I do?" Exasperation laced my voice, but I didn't know how to hide it. "She has plenty of friends." Like all of mine, for instance.

"She just ... I just ... Can't you try to be nicer to her?" Ruth asked.

"I've hardly spoken to her, Ruth. How is that upsetting her?"

"We all thought the two of you would be such good friends, and we built it up. I guess we shouldn't have. Is this really about Andrew? I didn't think you were like that, Sadie."

"Like what?"

"I don't know, all caught up in the drama. I told you that Andrew and Annabelle are just friends."

The conversation was fuzzy, dreamlike. Ruth should know me well enough not to say these things to me, but the words kept coming out of her mouth.

"You're acting so weird," Ruth said. "What's going on, Sadie?"

"I'm fine," I tried for a convincing smile.

"You're sure?" She eyed me carefully. "Because it's really important that—"

"What? That Annabelle's happy?" The last word came out with a bit of a snarl, so I adjusted my smile before I said, "I'm just tired today."

"Annabelle . . ." Ruth looked like she really wanted to tell me something but couldn't, for whatever reason. "She needs friends, that's all."

"What aren't you telling me?" I asked.

Ruth sighed. "Nothing. Never mind. Are you going to rehearsal tonight?"

"Yep," I said.

We turned to walk down the hallway, the silence deep between us.

Later, at rehearsal, I found Penny in her office collecting props.

"Oh perfect, Sadie. This stuff needs to go out to the Thompson's porch for the first scene."

I helped her carry the baskets and odds and ends for the cart outside.

"Sit anywhere," Penny said. "You'll be our guinea pig. For the show, we could put out chairs or picnic blankets or something, just so the audience sits in the right place."

Outside the Thompson's house, the obvious place to sit was the lawn, so I found a spot on the grass that didn't look too wet.

"Yep. We need picnic blankets." Penny sat next to me. "Or everyone's going to be walking around with wet bums."

Penny played the intro music on her iPhone, amplified by the portable speaker. As the song wound down, Ted sauntered into the yard, pulling an imaginary cart.

"So that's the cart you're building," Penny whispered. "It needs to be big enough to hold the music box and some boxes and bags—those can all be very light, filled with nothing—because the cart also has to be light enough for him to pull."

An impossible problem, but since we were talking about Ted who could lift a hundred-pound speaker over his head, maybe it wasn't such a big deal. The cart would be on wheels, too.

Ted knocked on the door and told Bea and Jasper, who played Annabelle's parents, that he had bad news. He was a surprisingly good actor, with the perfect mix of charm and creepiness that his character needed. I could see how the parents would believe him; but as an audience member, I still doubted that he was a good guy.

Annabelle's character was named Rose. Ted, supposedly the king's messenger, handed over the baskets of odds and ends that were supposed to be presents from the king. Then he took Rose by the hand and led her away from the cabin, while Rose's parents cried on one another's shoulders.

"That's our cue," Penny said as Ted headed out into the trees. "Someone will lead the audience to the next scene. We'll send them on a different path than the way Ted is going, so he can set up before they arrive."

We slowly walked along the audience's path, with Penny timing the walk. Penny described the tiki lanterns they planned to place along the path, and showed me how the trees and well-placed screens would block the audience's view of the actor's path.

Each scene in the forest built on the last one. In each new scene, dancers joined Rose's dreams, and she became more sad and hopeless. At the end of the sequence of three scenes, as the dance ended, Ruth helped Annabelle unbind her feet so she could escape into the woods.

We went to the last platform, which had been built on a rotating turntable. My storefronts would line the front, and then the platform would slowly spin around to show the inside of the bakery on the other side. Andrew's scene with Annabelle was coming up, and I couldn't watch it today. I showed my notes to Penny and whispered that I had to go.

"Don't you want to see the final scene and the dance?" she whispered back.

"I'll save it for next time." My voice quavered.

She grabbed my hand and squeezed. For a moment, I felt like the curtains had been pulled away, and Penny could see all the way inside of me. Something made me look back at her, hold her gaze.

"You're going to be okay, Sadie," she finally said, letting go of my hand. "I promise."

I blinked at her, trying to figure out what had just happened. People often said things like this; but for some reason, her words felt like a real promise. One I could count on. The promise stayed with me, solid and warm, as I walked back across the field.

You're going to be okay, Sadie.

From: Sadie Douglas
To: Pippa Reynolds
Date: Tuesday, April 17, 8:15 PM
Subject: Secrets

Everyone knows something about Annabelle that I don't know. I have no idea why they won't tell me, unless it's something to do with Andrew. But he seems to know about whatever it is, too. WHAT IS IT? They treat her like she's made of glass or something. Ruth told me I was hurting Annabelle's feelings, which is impossible, right? Even if I were, shouldn't Ruth be worried about my feelings too? Especially if the big secret is that Andrew likes Annabelle. ☹

Chapter 20

Sketches

After I hit Send, I stared, unseeing, at the computer screen. I should draw, since drawing usually settled my mind. Unfortunately, I didn't want to see what might come out on the page tonight. Two people lived inside of me—the one I was pretending to be, and the one I really was. And mostly, I just felt numb. The locked box I'd drawn floated in my mind, but I couldn't bear looking inside. Not tonight. The mess could stay at the bottom of the ocean, as far I was concerned.

I took out my sketchbook and pencils anyway. Not every drawing had to be complicated and intense, right? I traced the outline of a sphere. Pippa's hot air balloon. I'd draw it floating over a meadow. I sketched patterns on the balloon, and then I textured the grass. Still, the numbness didn't fade.

I can't feel.

No answers filled the silence. I closed my sketchbook. Drawing while I felt hollow like this was worse than not drawing at all. I curled up under the covers and made a space for Higgins. He lay next to me, and I buried my nose in his warm fur and waited for sleep to come.

School dragged on the next day. I ate lunch with Ruth and Annabelle and the others, and I tried to laugh and act normal, instead of like an empty shell. The only good part of the day was when Ruth agreed to help me with sets so I wouldn't have to work with Mr. Reid by myself.

After school, I had an art lesson with Vivian. On the drive to her house, the pocket watch that I'd slipped into my pocket that morning felt heavy. I still wasn't sure whether giving it to her was the right thing to do, and I didn't trust my judgment these days.

Vivian seemed busy, distracted, from the minute she opened the door. She wasn't her usual self today.

"I'm almost ready for the cement pour." She waved me toward the living room. "What do you think?"

Chicken-wire shapes crowded the small space.

"I don't usually work on more than one at a time." Vivian wandered around the room, touching a statue here and there. "But I'm trying to replicate what I had before."

I nodded, not sure what to say. I couldn't picture what these statues would look like, really, not when they were all crowded together and still made of only chicken wire. Of course, Vivian knew what she was doing, but the room looked more like a manufacturing line than the way Vivian's studio usually looked, with just one piece standing in the middle of the room. I remembered how she'd leave her current piece out, and touch it lovingly whenever she walked by, finding those places where she wanted to add color or texture. Sometimes she'd work on a sculpture for an entire month before moving on to the next one.

"Your dad offered to bring ceramic pieces from the old statues, salvaged from the yard. But I think I'll just run over to the thrift store and buy some new dishes to break."

"I told him you wouldn't want to dig shards out of your old stuff," I said.

Vivian bent the edge of one of the wire frames, pushing it into a tighter curve. "Usually, I *would* want to use the original pieces. But I have so little time, and I don't want to spend it wallowing in self-pity."

Maybe now. Is this the right time to give her the watch?

As I reached into my pocket and tried to get up my nerve, she said, "But you didn't come to talk about my statues. Let's take a look at those sketches."

Giving the watch to her later might be better. I took my drawings of the set pieces out of my backpack and laid them out on the floor, stepping back as she knelt down to take a look.

"How did you determine the measurements?" she asked.

"The wagon needs to hold the music box, and the music box needs to hold Annabelle, so I started with those dimensions."

"And you're worried about weight?"

"Ted is strong, but he needs to pull the cart on his own, at least until he's out of sight. Then, others can help him."

"Instead of doing a solid wood lid, you might want to consider using PVC piping and curtains for when the lid is up. You could make a false lid when it's closed ... would that work?" She sketched notes as she talked. "Luan is a thin wood you could paint and design exactly like your drawing, saving you a lot of weight. I suppose you could do the same with the sides of the box, just make a frame and make the outsides out of luan. You wouldn't need a bottom, right?"

"Yeah, I guess not."

Vivian turned to the next page — the storefronts — and frowned. "This is a lot of painting. Are you sure you have time to do all this?"

"Rose falls asleep on the bakery stoop and then goes inside, but I think we need something that looks like a street. We're using the cabin for the house at the beginning, but we need something like this at the end."

"It's just a lot ... all of these signs and windows and doors."

I nodded, not sure how to explain that I'd rather be busy painting during rehearsals, than watching Annabelle, or thinking about Mom, or wishing Ruth or Andrew would come talk to me.

Vivian looked at me, her eyes clear and no longer distracted. Neither of us had to say anything. We both knew why she had to create twenty statues at a time and I had to paint complicated scenes. We needed something to hold our attention, something to focus our energy and emotion. Being busy was better than either exploding with anger, or crumbling to pieces. Still, pressure continued to build inside me, every day, no matter how busy I made myself. Would I be able to keep holding it in? What would happen to me if I couldn't?

Vivian worked on measurements with me until Dad knocked on the door. I should have given her the pocket watch already because I didn't want to do it with Dad watching. I didn't know why. Now I'd have to wait for next time.

As I got into the Jeep, I could tell Dad wanted to tell me something. He kept opening his mouth to speak and then turning away.

After a few minutes of this, I said, "Why don't you just tell me whatever it is?"

He sighed. "It's Mom."

"What about Mom? She's okay, right?"

Dad ran his fingers through his hair. "She's coming home."

This was a problem? "So . . ."

"She didn't complete the treatment, and she's really discouraged. I think . . . I think we're in for a tough time."

As though it hadn't been tough already.

"What aren't you telling me?" I asked.

"I just want you to be ready, that's all. Mom has . . . well, she's decided she's not going to get better."

"But that isn't up to her," I said. "I mean, she'll get better or she won't, right?"

"Right. But if she gives up ..."

And then I finally understood what he was trying to say. Mom had given up. The realization hit me full speed, knocking the breath out of me.

"She'll be home on Friday," he said.

Dad didn't say anything else, and neither did I. There wasn't anything else to say.

From: Sadie Douglas
To: Frankie Paulson
Date: Wednesday, April 18, 6:45 PM
Subject: I'm a chicken

Yeah, I wanted to give Vivian the watch today, but I chickened out. I'll do it at my next lesson. I don't know. Maybe I can come to Vivian's art show. She has a lot to do still, but I think she'll have something to display. And I'd rather be in New York than at Annabelle Fest.

The drawing of your reflection in the water of that Alice in Wonderland statue was really amazing, Frankie. And sad. You look sad. Can I do anything to help you? I'll find a reflection of my own to draw and send it to you soon.

Tomorrow, I have to build sets with Mr. Reid (Annabelle's dad). Fortunately, Ruth promised to come too, so at least I won't have to be alone with him, listening to him go on and on about how perfect Annabelle is. Did I tell you he actually said that at dinner ... that she's perfect? Ugh.

From: Sadie Douglas
To: Pippa Reynolds
Date: Wednesday, April 18, 6:52 PM
Subject: :-(Happy Birthday

I miss you so much, Pips. I hope you had a perfect day.

Chapter 21

Sawdust

Sawdust filled the air as the blade whined through each board. I stood back while Mr. Reid cut the pieces for the music box.

"You're sure these measurements are going to work?" He turned off the saw and put his safety goggles on top of his head.

Where was Ruth? How could she have deserted me after she'd promised to be here?

Shrugging had become my fallback method of communication.

Mr. Reid raised an eyebrow. "Well, you did measure it all out, right? Because these are expensive boards. We wouldn't want to —"

"Yes." I finally found my voice. "I measured. And Vivian checked my work."

He shook his head. "What awful luck that woman had. Imagine a flood coming up so fast like that. Unpredictable."

"Thank you for cutting the boards for me." I was going to kill Ruth.

"Would almost make you feel like nature was singling you out."

Another shrug.

"You know, I tell Annabelle this all the time. Kids just don't know how great their lives are. You practically have no worries when you're a kid."

I circled around the boards and started brushing off the sawdust. Maybe if I started organizing them for my project, he'd stop lecturing.

"Annabelle tells me she worries about you because you never smile. You never smile? Now how can that be?"

He was like a dog with a bone that just wouldn't give up.

"Do you know that Annabelle actually thinks you're unhappy because of her?"

I set down my board louder than necessary. *Yes, actually. People keep telling me so.*

"That's not true, is it, Sadie?"

His gaze burned into the back of my head, and I knew I wouldn't get away without answering him. But maybe I could finally get out of the conversation too.

After staring at my toes for a few moments, I finally said, "I'm fine. I'm not unhappy. Umm ... I need to go get supplies."

I hurried away from the set-building area. As I got about

halfway across the field, I realized he might wait around to help me some more.

I turned back and shouted, "Thanks for your help, Mr. Reid. I can take it from here."

I ran the rest of the way to the church, through the sanctuary, and into the back hallway where Penny, Doug, and Ben's offices were. All I wanted was to escape, to hide, even from myself. At the end of the hall, I tried a door. Inside, Bibles and hymnals crowded a small supply cabinet. I went inside, closed the door, and breathed in the smell of ink and dust.

Tears spilled down my cheeks, slow and steady — not a storm this time. No matter how hard I tried, I couldn't pretend hard enough. Everyone saw through me. Even Annabelle's dad. It was like a current had swept me up, and I couldn't do anything to fight back. My own private flash flood. Only this flood went on and on and on.

"Sadie?" Ruth called from the hallway. "Penny said she thought you came in this way. Are you here?"

I considered staying in the closet, waiting until Ruth went away. But anger boiled up, hot and sudden. Ruth had left me to be lectured by Mr. Reid after she promised to be there for me. I threw open the door.

Ruth frowned at me. "Sadie, what were you doing in the — "

"Where were you?"

Ruth stepped back, away from me, from my angry words. "That's what I came to tell you. Annabelle scheduled a last-minute rehearsal for today since her dad was going to be here working anyway. She and Penny decided to add a dance after I untie Annabelle's feet—just for Annabelle and me. I didn't even know I could dance before Annabelle started teaching me—What is it, Sadie?"

The hallway was dark, but she must have finally noticed my tear-streaked face.

"You promised you'd be there to help me."

"Yes, but … I thought you'd understand, Sadie." Her voice faltered. "I thought you'd be happy for me."

I couldn't answer. I sat down and put my head in my hands.

"Mr. Reid did all the cutting, right? I mean, you didn't need me for anything."

Tears poured out of me, hot acid sizzling down my cheeks.

"Sadie, I don't understand what's wrong with you lately. You were obviously miserable at lunch these last few days."

I couldn't breathe.

"You're not giving Annabelle a chance at all. And the play is supposed to be fun, but you're …." Ruth knelt down by me. Her sleeve brushed my cheek as she put her hand on my shoulder.

"Sadie, can't you just try to be happy?"

Instead of bursting out, my anger exploded deep inside me, shattering every bit of fight I had left. I felt like she'd pushed me into deep, inky water. Coldness slithered through my body, and I sunk down inside myself so that her next words rippled on their way to my ears. Her hand felt like dead weight on my shoulder.

"Just try, Sadie."

I nodded because it was the only thing I could think to do. And then I stood up, in my newly watery body. Every step felt like it took the last bit of energy I had.

Ruth frowned at me and then checked the clock on the wall. "I have to get back to rehearsal. Will you be okay, Sadie?"

I nodded again and then watched her bounce down the hallway, her question hanging in the air between us. My feet felt as heavy as rocks as I walked out to the steps to wait for Dad, trying not to think about Mom coming home tomorrow. Worse and worse and worse.

Chapter 22

Breathe

After Dad dropped me off from school, he went to pick up Mom at the airport. She was paler than ever when she walked through the door, holding tightly to Dad's arm.

"She needs a little sleep," Dad said. "And then we can have dinner together."

Mom barely looked at me as he took her upstairs.

I went up to my room and lay down on the bed. Higgins tried to lick my face, but I pushed him away. I stared at the ceiling until the lines and knots started forming pictures, waves and wind and angry faces staring down at me. I closed my eyes. Was this how Mom felt all the time, like even sitting up would require too much strength?

Dad called me down to dinner later, and I didn't know if I'd slept or not. I could have been lying there forever or for just a few minutes. I forced myself to stand up, walk across the room, and go downstairs, step after step.

Mom sat at the table and looked out the window. I don't know what I'd expected. Dad had tried to warn me. Still, seeing Mom like this, totally drained of life, was worse than any time she'd been sick before. Now it wasn't that she couldn't hold her head up or couldn't keep her eyes open. She was just ... gone. Even though her body was here. I didn't know how to bring her back, if that was even possible. I stood there, just watching her for a while, until Dad poked his head out of the kitchen.

"Come help me, Sades?"

I helped Dad carry salad and soup to the table. As we ate, Dad asked me to tell Mom the story of the spirit bear, and then he asked me questions about the set pieces and the play. He told Higgins stories, and I tried to laugh. Mom smiled every once in a while, but she didn't come back to herself.

Finally, as we were taking last bites, Dad said, "We're happy to have you home, Cindy."

"I missed you," she said, her voice no more than a whisper.

I looked at my fork. Why could I still not feel anything? The numbness frightened me. I stood up and started clearing dishes, the burst of energy taking me by surprise.

"Thanks, Sades," Dad said.

I hurried off to the kitchen and made as much noise as I could washing dishes, battling the terrible silence that had settled over the house.

By the time I was finished, Dad had taken Mom upstairs

again. I called good night to them on the stairs and went to my room. Too quiet. I couldn't email anyone right now because what would I say? Finally, I took out my sketchbook. Maybe tonight I could finally feel something when I drew.

The white page glowed in the moonlight. Where to start?

I can't do this.

Are you out there?

What's wrong with me?

The silence was heavy. My mind was as blank as Vivian's apartment walls.

I know you're out there.

Why won't you answer me?

I tossed my sketchbook aside and threw myself onto my bed, burying my face in the pillows. Higgins whined, jumped onto the bed, and nudged me with his nose. I should scratch his ears, but I couldn't lift my arm. My eyes were dry. My entire body ached. I felt as though giant hands had grabbed me and started to squeeze; if I couldn't get free, I would die. But minute after minute passed, and I lay there, gasping for breath.

Breathe.

Just one word, and I knew it hadn't come from my own mind. At that moment I was about as capable of telling myself to breathe as I was of lifting Dad's Jeep over my head. It wasn't the answer I'd hoped for, but I didn't actually know what I wanted. I wanted God to fix everything. And I couldn't even put "everything" into words.

I rolled over onto my back and hugged a pillow to my

chest, practicing the breathing Mom and I used to do in yoga. In through the mouth, out through the nose. Slower. In. Out. In. Out. Breath after breath after breath.

Just let me go to sleep. Give me that at least.

Tomorrow, I had to go to school. Had to see Ruth, Annabelle. I just needed ... what?

Breathe. The instruction came again.

So I kept breathing. In. Out. And with my eyes closed, I started to see something new. As I breathed in, the air was silver, shimmery, like liquid starlight slipping up into my nose and down my throat. As it swirled into my lungs, it cooled the ragged pain. As I breathed out, inky blackness poured out into the night, like poison draining out of a snakebite.

In. Out. In. Out.

I'm breathing starlight. And something is coming out of me.

Breathe.

I should draw.

Breathe.

The word wrapped around the starlight. I kept breathing as I climbed under the covers, as I arranged my pillows, as Higgins curled up next to me. I kept breathing as I fell into a dream where stars, like lily pads, led me out into the night sky.

Chapter 23

Too Tired to Cry

Dad dropped me off early for the work party. I wanted to get there before everyone else so I could set up the paint and wood without an audience. Everything seemed to take me twice as long now, too, so I appreciated the extra time. And, I'd wanted to escape Mom.

Today, we'd work on constructing the music box and the cart, and then give each piece a base coat.

If Mr. Reid came back, or if Doug had time to work the saw, we'd also cut pieces for the storefronts. Penny was in charge of the costume projects today, and Ben was going to do all the props. So I'd only have to manage four or five people, which was good.

The air was cool and smelled like dew as I walked across the field to the picnic table and benches that had become my set-construction station. We'd piled the wood on bricks and covered it with tarps to keep it as dry as possible. A collection of paint cans, brushes, and extra tarps waited on the table. They'd taken all the power tools inside. I laid out the tarp and started sorting the wood into piles, one for the cart, one for the music box, and another for the bakery oven and countertop.

I was so busy measuring boards and comparing them to my notes, I didn't hear Andrew come up behind me.

"Hey there," he said.

I almost jumped out of my skin. I whirled around to face him.

"Didn't mean to scare you." His smile made my heart leap around in my chest. "Thought I'd come early to see if you needed help."

"Um, yeah." I scanned the yard. Just me and Andrew and no one else. I'd managed to avoid him pretty well for the week. But now I had no excuses.

"I'm just sorting the wood into piles."

Andrew grabbed the other end of a board I was about to pick up, so I wouldn't have to drag it through the grass. We worked in silence that became more uncomfortable by the second.

After we set down the last board, I wiped off my hands. "I guess I'll go get the tools."

I almost got away, but he grabbed my arm.

"Wait, Sadie," he said. "I want to talk to you."

Here it was. I didn't want to have this conversation no matter where it led.

"About Annabelle, I mean."

Especially not if it was about Annabelle.

"You're really hurting her feelings, Sades. I mean, she doesn't understand why you won't talk to her, and we're all starting to worry because ..."

"Because why?" I asked. I was tired of all the secrets. If something was wrong with Annabelle, someone needed to come out and tell me so.

Andrew opened his mouth and then, as though he'd suddenly changed his mind, he closed it again.

I pressed on. "As far as I can see, Annabelle is fine. She's the lead in the play. Everyone loves her. She never stops smiling. I have no idea why everyone's so worried about her."

"Sadie, she—"

"I get it. You all love her." The word practically stuck in my throat, but I pushed it out. "I don't understand why I can't just stay out of your way. Why do I have to be Annabelle's best friend too?"

"Annabelle was sick last year. Really sick. She ended up going into the hospital because she didn't eat."

I shook my head, not understanding. "Why didn't she eat? What does this have to do with me?"

"She ate only gummy peaches, Sadie. For months. And she still thought she was fat when she was just skin and bones. We were all so happy to see her healthy and happy, we just didn't want anything to upset that. And you—"

"Wait. Are you saying she's not eating again now? And you're blaming that on me?"

"I'm saying that you're hurting her. And she's not the kind of person people should hurt."

"What about me? Is it fine for everyone to go around hurting me?"

Andrew frowned. "Who's hurting you?"

"My point exactly," I said. "People are coming, and I need to get the tools."

As I walked away, he called after me, "Sadie, I'm serious. Who's hurting you?"

I turned back to look at him, to see if he was serious. He looked truly baffled as he closed the distance between us.

"Never mind," I finally said.

"Sadie, out of everyone around here, I thought you'd be the best friend for Annabelle. And I told her so. I made her think the two of you would be perfect together. But you're acting so ... I wouldn't think you'd be so mean."

"Mean?" The word came out as a snarl. I couldn't help it. How could he not see what was going on?

"Yes, *mean*, Sadie."

I couldn't come up with anything to say. Not a single thing. I turned and walked away, leaving him standing there, calling after me.

"What's going on, Sadie?" Bea asked, passing me on her way to the costume station.

"Nothing," I said, not stopping.

After I passed, I heard her say to Lindsay, "What's her problem?"

Lindsay answered, "I don't know. She's been mean to everyone lately."

Mean. That's what I was now. Mean to everyone. Still, the tears wouldn't come. I was too tired to cry.

From: Sadie Douglas
To: Frankie Paulson
Date: Sunday, April 22, 4:21 PM
Subject: Soon

I'll draw my reflection picture soon, Frankie. I promise.

Thanks for the drawing of Georgiana with her morning hair sticking up every which way. It did make me laugh. I'm not sure I'll be able to top that. I'll talk to Vivian about coming with her to New York and let you know, okay?

Chapter 24

Poetry

Sun streamed through the classroom windows, and the glare off my desk made me squint. "Just one idea," Ms. Barton had said as she explained the poetry assignment. But none of the ideas in my head were appropriate for a poem. Poetry flowed when you read it out loud, each word sliding into the next. My words were more likely to stab, gashing holes in this dumb worksheet. So to begin:

IMAGES THAT COME TO MIND WHEN YOU CLOSE YOUR EYES.

Mud. Broken fish. White walls. Cracked roof. Freckled nose. Gummy peaches. Mom staring out the window. My mean face.

FEELINGS THAT COME TO MIND:

Nope. Not going there.

SHAPE THESE WORDS INTO A POEM:

It's

Not

Fair.

The bell rang and I crumpled up my notebook page and threw it into the recycling bin.

"Sadie—" Ms. Barton reached into the bin and pulled out my paper.

I snatched it away from her. "Don't read it."

She stared at me and only then did it cross my mind that I shouldn't have ripped my paper out of my teacher's hand. I knew I should say something, but the words caught in my throat, so I ran for the door.

"Hey, Sadie," Ruth caught my arm as I came into the hallway. "Andrew told me he told you. About Annabelle, I mean."

I blinked at her, my heart still thudding in my chest. She glanced over her shoulder, but Annabelle was still in the classroom talking to Abby and Erin. "Now do you understand?"

I fidgeted with my backpack and clothes, anything so I didn't have to look her in the eye.

"I should have told you, I know. But I promised Annabelle I wouldn't. She just wanted to be friends with you on normal terms, not have you know her as the girl who got sick last summer."

"So you blame me, too, for her being upset or not eating or whatever?"

"I just think we'd be a lot happier if we could all hang out together. I miss you, Sades."

Annabelle caught up with us and smiled her Annabelle smile. "Where are you sitting at lunch today, Sadie?"

She must be exhausted, keeping this up all the time. I didn't understand, though, why someone who seemed to have everything wouldn't eat. What did she have to punish herself for?

Ruth looked from Annabelle, who was all smiles, to me. All frowns, I'm sure.

"You choose. I'll be over in a second," Ruth said.

As Annabelle walked away, Ruth turned to me. "Just try being happy today, Sadie. You'll have fun, I promise."

"And Annabelle will be happy." My voice was flat.

Too many feelings had raced through me for the past few days. Guilt, frustration, jealousy that everyone was worried about Annabelle and not worried about me, loneliness, and so much more that I couldn't even begin to sort it all out. I didn't know how I could sit through lunch with Ruth and Annabelle again and pretend that everything was okay.

Ruth blinked at me, as though she didn't understand how I could still be upset. "Well, yeah, Sades, she will. That's a good thing."

Whatever I said would only make me sound worse.

Finally, I shook my head. "No thanks. I've got some homework to catch up on anyway. I'll be in the library."

"Sadie ..." Ruth sounded like she was about to begin a lecture on how unreasonable I was being.

I shrugged and gave her a sad smile. "I just need a little time, Ruth. Okay?"

Something in my voice stopped her, because she tilted her head and her eyebrows pulled into a confused frown, as though she'd been looking at an optical illusion a certain way for a long time, and then suddenly she saw the negative space, the opposite point of view.

"Sadie . . . ?" Ruth said again, but this time my name was more of a question.

"It's fine, Ruth," I said. "We'll talk more later, okay?"

I didn't wait for her to answer before I walked down the hall. I felt her watching me until I turned the corner. I knew we'd have to talk at some point. But not today.

Chapter 25

Lost or Found

Dad dropped me off at Vivian's house after school on Wednesday, telling me to invite Vivian over for dinner afterward.

I walked across the parking lot and up Vivian's stairs. Lifting my hand to knock on the door felt like lifting my backpack full of textbooks. Maybe something *is* wrong with me. Maybe chronic fatigue syndrome is hereditary, and now I'm getting it too. Or maybe I'm one of those people who suddenly go insane in the middle of seventh grade. I'd heard about cases like that on the news, on some TV special report.

Vivian opened her door. For a second, my watery vision sharpened. Vivian looked terrible, with dark circles under her eyes and rumpled clothes. Her house had a closed-up, stuffy smell, and over her shoulder I could see dirty laundry, clutter, and dishes scattered around. She looked exactly the way I felt.

"Come in," Vivian finally said. "I forgot about your lesson, but I'm glad you're here."

She kicked some laundry aside as we walked down the hall, and then she cleared a seat for me on a chair in the living-room-turned-art-studio.

Since last week, she'd created a number of new chicken-wire forms, which looked like they might be the trees she was planning to use as part of the exhibit.

"I need to finish them. I have to pour the concrete and do the ceramic work," she said. "For a few days there, all I did was work. But then ..." She raised her hands helplessly.

I wandered around the room, trying to picture how the sculptures would look when they were finished. She easily had twenty figures in the room, and I had no idea how she was going to finish them all in a little more than a week.

"A few days ago, the insurance claims adjuster brought me pictures of the cleanup work at my house," Vivian said. "Not many photos, but enough so I could see how ... gone ... everything is. And something inside of me just broke. I haven't been able to work ever since."

I nodded.

"But I promised you, Sadie. I'm sorry. I just don't think ..."

I forced myself to find words, to form them, to say them. "Me, neither."

She frowned at me, frowned at the room, and seemed to finally notice something was off. "I should open a window."

As she pushed the window open as high as it would go, a slight breeze came in and lifted tiny particles into the air, swirling them in the sunlight so they shimmered like magic dust. I watched them dance in the air, so light and free and beautiful. Why couldn't I decide to let all of this go? Ruth wanted me to, Andrew wanted me to, and Mom probably wanted me to, as well. "Just be happy," they'd all say. "Stop worrying so much about everything."

What's wrong with me? And where are you?

Vivian stood at the window, breathing in the fresh air. When she turned, her cheeks were wet with tears. She wiped them away and smiled a sad smile.

"Sadie, we're both a mess." She gestured around the room. "Literally and figuratively."

"I tried to work," I told her. "I tried to pretend everything was okay, but ..." I wished the tears would come, but I couldn't cry anymore.

"Yeah, I know." She sat across from me. "When David died, I thought I was crazy. I honestly thought I was losing my mind. First, I was angry, and then suddenly I had all of this energy to get things done. But one day, I couldn't feel anything anymore. Like now. Sadness, pain, loss—they were a fog wrapped all around me, getting thicker every day. Everyone else acted normal, as if they couldn't see that I was being buried alive by my emotions. Or they demanded that I try harder—cheer up and get back to work. I couldn't. And I can't now, either."

"What happened?" I asked. "Back then, I mean."

"When you're in the middle of it," Vivian said, "You want things to be different. You want to feel better, but you know that trying to feel better only leads to more pain. And I know you now understand what I'm talking about because you just tried it."

"But one day, Peter came home with three fish — red fish — and two things happened: I wanted to take care of those fish. I also wanted to paint them, just the way they were. There was something about the color red — a color I couldn't figure out how to mix. So I got busy drawing up plans for an aquarium built right inside the wall, and I painted those fish who temporarily lived in a glass bowl in my art studio. And somehow, once the aquarium was installed and the fish painting was complete, I felt as though someone had opened a window."

"And you could breathe again."

"Yes. But I couldn't have gotten there on my own, Sadie."

"I wish I could help you."

"Why don't you tell me what's going on with you? I know it's not just my house that's gotten you to this place, right?"

So I told her everything leaving no horrible detail unsaid — even though I knew I sounded like the worst person in the world. And as I told her, something shifted inside of me. I realized I still cared about sending scavenger hunt updates to Frankie. I wanted to be there for her — not because it was a "good thing to do," but because I wanted to do it. I also wanted to finish the music box for the play because I wanted to see something that I'd imagined in my mind come to life in the real world.

"I've been keeping something from you," I said.

"What's that?" Vivian asked.

I took the watch out of my pocket and held it out to her. "I found this in the woods on the day we worked at your house."

She reached out, her fingers shaking, and took the watch. After tracing the initials on the back, she opened the cover and then clicked it closed again.

"I gave this to David as a wedding present," she said. "He lost it when Andrew was little—only five or six years old. We used to play Find The Pocket Watch, scouring the forest looking for it. But we never found it."

"It was almost completely buried in the underbrush," I said. "I'd never have seen it if I wasn't trying to find 'something abandoned' for Frankie's scavenger hunt."

"It's funny how you can lose one thing and gain something else, isn't it?" Vivian curled her fingers around the watch and looked out the window. For a minute it was almost as if she'd left the room.

"Vivian?" I asked after a pause, prepared to apologize for upsetting her with the watch. I'd been afraid it would upset her more.

Vivian smiled. "Sorry. I left you there for a minute, didn't I? I've been thinking about the centerpiece for my collection since I left New York. My vague idea was one large tree in the middle—part sculpture, and part tree. I've been calling it "The Grandfather Tree" in my mind. But what if the tree held memories? I could use objects, such as this watch and other important items, as part of the tree."

"I love it!" I said.

"I don't have too many objects like that one, but I do have some that your dad found when he dug around at the house." Vivian suddenly gasped. "Or maybe—grab your coat."

Chapter 26

You Are My Sunshine

Followed Vivian out to the truck. Her newfound energy was contagious. As I opened the truck door, I realized I'd nearly run across the parking lot just now; when only an hour ago, my feet had been too heavy to lift. Up and down and up and down, my emotions were completely unpredictable. Even though I was happy not to be down right now, I still felt a little nuts.

"I can't believe I didn't think of this before," Vivian said as she pulled onto the main road. "You're not going to believe it. Wait." She slowed the truck. "What time is your dad coming to pick you up?"

"He said we could take as long as we wanted. And he invited you to join us for dinner, too."

"That's sweet. But after this, I don't think I'll want to do anything but work. I figured out the missing piece." Vivian turned the truck onto a gravel road and we skidded a bit as she rounded the first corner.

"Sorry, I'll slow down. I just can't wait for . . ." She slowed the truck again and craned her neck to look back into the trees.

I looked too, but I saw nothing; so I was shocked when she shouted, "There!" and slammed on the brakes.

"Where?" I squinted but still didn't see anything.

"It's a little ways in. Let's go look."

We hiked along a poorly marked, overgrown trail, jumping over logs and wading through wet patches until we stepped into a clearing, I now felt the same way I had when I'd seen the spirit bear: As though I'd just stumbled into a dream. A grand piano and a bench, covered with trailing ivy, were just sitting there as though someone had prepared a concert for the forest dwellers.

"What . . . ?" I began.

"Olivia Wendelson's husband couldn't bear the thought of visiting his wife in the cemetery, but he wanted to preserve her memory somewhere. So he bought this plot of land and put her piano out here. For a few years, people came to visit it all the time; but now it's all but forgotten, I think. At least I'd forgotten about it until today."

"Does it still play?" I asked.

"It probably doesn't sound very good, but I do think it still plays," she said. "Try it."

I circled the piano feeling quiet and a little shy, but I really, really wanted to play it. Finally, I sat on the bench and ran my fingers over the keys. My reflection stared back at me wide-eyed and full of wonder from the shiny black surface. How it could still be shiny after all this time, I had no idea. I smiled. I'd found my reflection picture for Frankie.

I'd memorized only three songs during my piano lesson days, but as I looked at the piano with the sun streaming down on the ivy, I knew what song to play.

"You Are My Sunshine" came out warbled and out of tune, but the notes ran together in an oddly magical way, filling the clearing and slipping under my skin.

Vivian stood with her eyes closed until I finished. "It will be perfect for the center of my exhibit. Not a tree—but a piano. And inside the ivy that's crawling all over the piano, treasured memories will be tucked away."

"Can I help?" I asked.

"You need to work on your set pieces for the play. But you can stay over tonight and help me—if your dad says it's okay."

I called Dad on the drive back, and he agreed to let me stay over. The rest of the evening was a flurry of work. We managed to build the piano with chicken wire and stretched fabric, and we also created wire ivy vines and some fabric leaves. We hadn't eaten by eleven o'clock, so Vivian called to order takeout.

"Would it be okay if I went back to New York with you? For the exhibit?" I asked.

"Isn't that the same night as your play?" she asked.

"Yeah, but . . . I'm not really sure I want to . . . I don't know."

"If you want to come with me, you're welcome to. But consider staying for the show. You've worked so hard, and seeing it all come together would be really special."

I took a bite of pizza that was still so hot the cheese stretched out in long threads. "I can work on the leaves this week, if you want me to. And maybe I can get some people to help at rehearsals, during downtime. 'Cause you'll need a lot of leaves—for the trees and the ivy on the piano."

"Only if you have time," Vivian said. "Actually, let's make a pact."

"About what?" I asked.

"Let's both promise not to bury ourselves in work to try to avoid our feelings—like we did before."

"Yeah, so we're making a pact not to work?" I asked.

"We're making a pact to be artists. By now you know the difference between working and creating. I do too, but I've been so busy working that I haven't allowed myself to create."

"I haven't been able to draw in my sketchbook either," I said. "It just feels … empty."

"That's what I mean. How have you felt tonight?" she asked.

I hadn't been thinking about how I felt, actually, which was the opposite of what I'd been doing for the past few weeks. Until tonight, all I'd done was think about how miserable I was.

"I want to draw." I took my last bite of pizza and threw away my paper plate and napkin.

Vivian had bought an inexpensive bed, but she still had the air mattress we'd brought out for her. So she set it up in the living room.

"You're sure you don't want to sleep in the bedroom?" she asked.

"No, this is perfect."

Vivian set my two canvases side by side, the waves and the swinging girl. I piled up the pillows so I could lean against them and draw, facing the canvases. I turned to an empty page in my sketchbook.

I divided the page into eight squares and started sketching. First, I drew the box at the bottom of the ocean and a dolphin swimming by. Then I drew the key. In the next box, I drew the key being tossed on the waves. Then, the key was up in the air being carried by the wind. The key soared over trees, through clouds, past the nose of a spirit bear, and came to rest on top of a forgotten piano.

I looked back at the drawing of the locked box. I still wasn't ready to open it yet, but tomorrow I'd tell Vivian that I'd accept her pact. I would try my best to be an artist. Because even when I didn't have any answers—even when I felt confused and frustrated and lost—drawing helped me to see new possibilities.

I closed my sketchbook and went to look out the window. *I'm here.*

"Thank you," I whispered.

Chapter 27

Ruth's Song

The next day at rehearsal, I dipped my brush into the gold paint and began tracing my pencil lines. The metallic swirls stood out against the vivid green of the box, the perfect compliment. Everyone else was busy running through the show, so I could lose myself in the painting.

Across the field, Cameron and the band started playing Ruth and Annabelle's song. I knew the music, but I hadn't actually seen their dance. Was I being selfish? It was like Ruth and I were on opposite sides of a brick wall; each of us pushed, but neither of us seemed able to knock down the barrier. No matter how much we shouted to one another about how things looked from our own side of the wall, neither of us could see the other side.

The music stopped abruptly, mid-song. They'd start again, probably, once they'd worked out some detail or another. I stifled a groan. I couldn't avoid it. Maybe I couldn't see things from Ruth's perspective, but as long as I sat around nursing a grudge and refusing to be there for her since she hadn't been there for me, I was making things worse between us. I'd made a pact with Vivian not to work harder, but to create. I couldn't create as long as I held on to all of this anger.

I rinsed my brush in the water bucket and left it there to soak. The music started up again when I was halfway across the field. As I got closer, through the trees I saw a skirt twirl here and a hand extend there. Once I'd passed into the clearing, I stopped to watch. Ruth had taken on some of Annabelle's glow. Her arms moved in graceful arcs as she leapt and spun. The dance was a call-and-response. Ruth danced, and then Annabelle responded with movement of her own.

Annabelle hadn't taken out any of the turns in this dance. Clearly, Ruth knew some secret to turning, or else Annabelle had taught her well, because at the end of the dance, they went into a sequence where Ruth spun in looping circles around Annabelle, faster and faster until I felt dizzy just watching her. When they finally stopped, they each held up an arm and looked straight up, mirror images of one another. Then, surrounded by a cloud of fog and through a well-placed trapdoor in the bottom of the platform we'd built for this scene, Ruth disappeared.

She came out from under the platform to watch the rest of the scene — something she wouldn't be able to do during the actual show. No one expected her to stay curled up in the dark during rehearsal, though. The minute she saw me standing there, she stopped and looked confused. I smiled and gave her a thumbs-up, nodding toward where she'd danced just moments before. She came over to me, her expression still tentative.

"I thought you were painting."

"I heard your music and decided to take a break. Amazing, by the way."

She looked at me then, hope and worry mixed on her face. "Do you really think so? I got a few of the steps wrong ..."

"No one would have known, Ruth. I had no idea you could dance like that."

"Annabelle's a really good teacher—" Ruth stopped as though she'd said something wrong.

Ruth and I were never careful around one another. This wasn't what we did. We told each other what we thought; we argued stuff out. We didn't do this careful, polite thing. I smiled at her, but I didn't force the sadness out of it.

"And you're a really good dancer. I'm sorry it took me so long to come see you."

Now it was Ruth's turn to smile sadly. We both knew what she was about to say, and I stopped her before she said it.

"It's not okay, Ruth. Not really."

"Shhh!" Claudia hissed at us, which brought real smiles to our faces.

"I'd better get back to painting," I told her.

"I'll come help after rehearsal sometime, if you want me to. Or I can just keep you company or whatever. We both know I'm not the best artist in the world."

"Good thing, too. I've got to save one talent for myself if you're going to be the dancing-singing-acting queen."

"Shhh!" Claudia hissed again, even though we were whispering now.

Ruth and I did identical eye rolls and then grinned at each other.

"See ya."

"See ya."

My grin lasted all the way back to the music box.

After rehearsal, Ruth, Bea, and Lindsay stopped by the set-design station.

"Is there anything we can do to help?" Ruth asked. "My mom's waiting for me with the twins now, but I can help after rehearsal on Saturday, if you want. I'll bring paint clothes."

Bea and Lindsay watched me with tentative smiles, like they expected me to start shouting any minute. "Actually, if any of you would like to help Vivian, she needs some help more than I do."

"With what?" Bea asked.

"She's making a piano covered with ivy for her exhibit, and a bunch of trees. So she needs a bajillion leaves made of fabric. I've been cutting some out, but if you wanted to take some fabric and patterns—"

"Fun!" Bea lost her worried expression and clapped her

hands. "We'd be helping with a real New York City art exhibit!"

As I wiped off my hands and passed out fabric to the girls, I noticed Andrew watching me while he walked across the field with Cameron. He looked away as soon as he caught my eye, but not before a half-smile crossed his face.

Bea and Lindsay left with their armfuls of fabric, but Ruth hung back. "I heard your mom came home, Sadie. How is she?"

I almost shrugged, but stopped myself. "Not so good."

"I'm sorry," Ruth said. "I've been so busy thinking about the play and Annabelle that ... well, I'm sorry."

A car honked.

"You'd better run," I nodded toward the parking lot, "so your mom says yes about helping on Saturday."

"Right." Ruth gathered up her things and jogged off.

I should feel better now that Ruth and I were talking again. And while I still didn't know what was going on between Andrew and me, that didn't feel like the real issue — the numbness that wasn't going away. Any minute now, the floor could drop out from under me, and I'd turn into "crazy Sadie" all over again.

"Need help with those brushes, Sadie?" Penny asked, walking past me on her way back to the office.

I remembered her promise that I was going to be okay, and I wanted to ask her to stay, to tell me how she could be so sure that was true. But I thought I knew what she'd say. Just like the dancing girl in the bakery in our play, I'd have to find my own song, my own dance. And maybe it was enough to know that people like Penny believed I could. One day.

"I've got it. But thanks!" I said and then hurried to finish because Dad would be waiting for me.

And Mom. But I'd worry about her later.

From: Sadie Douglas
To: Frankie Paulson
Date: Thursday, April 26, 8:41 PM
Subject: A Concert for Forest Dwellers

I gave the pocket watch to Vivian, and it reminded her of the piano in these pictures I've attached. It's a real piano sitting out in the woods—and it still plays. Can you believe it? So Vivian made a piano just like it (but out of fabric and chicken wire, of course) to be the center of her art show, with treasures tucked into the ivy.

Vivian and I talked about my coming to the show with her, and Dad says I can. So it looks like I'll be back in New York very soon! Send me some more drawings.

From: Sadie Douglas
To: Pippa Reynolds
Date: Thursday, April 26, 8:53 PM
Subject: RE: WHERE ARE YOU????

Sorry, sorry, sorry, Pips. I miss you too.

I found out why everyone was protecting Annabelle. She starved herself last summer, but I have no idea why. So now everyone is all worried that she's not eating again. At first I was really upset because it seemed like Andrew and Ruth and everyone else were blaming me for it. But I had an okay conversation with Ruth today. And I don't know what to think about Andrew. I can't figure out why someone as perfect as Annabelle, who has everything she could possibly want, wouldn't eat. What's that about?

Mom is home now and still really sick; but mostly she's unhappy, I think. She just stares out the window or lies in bed. I can't feel anything about her at all, Pips. Not sad or mad or frustrated or anything. It scares me.

Send me some good news about you.

Chapter 28

Elements

Ruth smiled at me as I slipped in, almost late, to class. I took out my notebook and pencil as quietly as I could, as Ms. Barton started talking.

"On Monday, I asked you to write a poem, but I didn't give you much guidance—just to see what you'd do. Well, your poems ranged from humorous to practical to deep and meaningful."

"The meaningful one was my ode to pepperoni pizza," Mario called out.

"I put yours in the humorous pile, actually." Ms. Barton smiled. "Here's my point: Poems can be any of those things—silly, serious, you name it. So we're going to spend some time working on poems from prompts. You can take them in whatever direction you'd like."

"What about—" Mario began.

"As long as you keep it appropriate for school," Ms. Barton interrupted.

My mind was filled with thoughts about Mom, but I couldn't write a poem about her — not when I had no idea how I felt.

"I'd like you to choose a natural element to compare yourself to. It could be a force of nature or something you find outside. Use descriptive language and poetic form to show why you and this element are alike."

"I don't get it," Abby said.

Erin leaned over to whisper an explanation, but Ms. Barton interrupted. "Thank you, Erin, for your help. But maybe we could all use an example? I'll read you a poem that I love."

She flipped open a worn, leather book and turned to a page she'd marked. The poem she read was about how the poet felt like an ink pot — sometimes so dried up that the words just wouldn't come. Other times he overflowed with so many words that he couldn't write them down fast enough.

"Now, an ink pot isn't a natural object," Ms. Barton said, closing the book. "But notice how the poet uses adjectives and draws out the metaphor? That's what I want you to do."

I closed my eyes, but no images came to mind. Ms. Barton circled the room. She'd probably think I was fooling around if she found me drawing, but I wasn't sure how else to come up with an image. I didn't want a repeat of the crumpled poem from Monday. Ms. Barton seemed to be in a relatively good mood this morning, so I might as well give drawing a try.

As soon as my pencil touched the page, ideas started to flow. I sketched quickly, giving myself plenty of options. A tree wasn't right. Not a flower either, or a river, a waterfall, a volcano.

Ms. Barton stopped at my desk. "How are those ideas coming today, Sadie?"

"I think I'm getting closer."

She smiled. "Great. Good work."

Maybe it only bothered her when I drew during math. Fair enough, since my drawings had absolutely nothing to do with math, and we both knew I was only avoiding the tangle of numbers. As I relaxed into my drawing, I found myself sketching a key tumbling in the wind.

And then I knew what to write my poem about.

It came out in a flurry of words—so fast that I didn't feel like I was thinking. I was catching the words as they poured through me, the same way my pictures sometimes did when I drew at night.

> What if the wind
> could choose
> whether
> to bluster or breeze
> to swirl or storm
> to lilt or lie still
> But the wind cannot choose
> Instead, the sun

The moon
The angle of the earth
Combine
Outside pressures
The wind cannot control
Like me
The wind wakes up
Only to discover
What others have planned
Still, maybe she chooses
Sometimes.

When the bell rang, I waited until everyone had turned in their poems before I walked up to Ms. Barton's desk with mine.

As I handed her my poem, I said, "I'm sorry about the other day. I wasn't feeling very 'poem-y.'"

Ms. Barton smiled and tapped her fingers on the stack of poems on her desk. "I thought that might be the case. May I read this now?"

When I nodded, she looked down at my poem. Her lips moved as she read down the page.

"You know what?" Ms. Barton said, finally looking up. "I really hope she does get to choose some of the time."

I nodded again, feeling the heaviness lift a little more. All of these tiny choices—writing the poem instead of blowing it off, watching Ruth dance instead of pretending to be too busy with my sets—might not change anything around me, but they changed *me*. And maybe that was enough.

"Nice work today, Sadie," Ms. Barton said.

"Thank you." I smiled and headed for PE.

During rehearsal, I touched up the gold flourishes on the music box as I waited for Annabelle. I'd rather do almost anything than spend a half hour with her, explaining how to use the box. But since I'd made it, it would be weird if I asked someone else to help her. Then she'd have yet another reason to think I hated her.

She gasped behind me. "Sadie, this is beautiful!"

I turned to face her, half expecting to see a sarcastic expression on her face. But instead, she stared openmouthed at the box. I should have expected a genuine reaction from Annabelle. I'd never heard her use sarcasm before. She was too perfect for sarcasm.

She reached toward the box.

"Careful. Some of the paint is still wet."

My voice must have been sharper than I intended because she flinched and stepped back. "I'm sorry."

"I didn't mean ..."

She shook her head like it didn't matter, but some of the light had gone out of her eyes. Her smile was just as bright as ever, though.

Maybe she really did care what I thought, although I couldn't imagine why.

"Do you want me to show you how to use the box?" I asked, hoping the change in subject would make this conversation less awkward.

"Yeah, sure," she said.

I demonstrated how to fold back the false top at the hinges and slide it down into the box, and how to set up the pipes with the curtains so the box looked open. We practiced until we could do the change from closed to open in thirty seconds, and from open to closed in the same amount of time.

"It's almost like a dance," she said as we set the lid down for the last time.

I checked my watch. "Twenty-nine seconds."

"We'll never have to do it so quickly during the show," Annabelle said. "I think all of the scene changes will allow for at least a minute. People will be moving on the trails, and Doug is leading the group, trying to make it take five minutes for each walk."

"I probably won't be there to help you during the show, so you'll have to teach someone else how to do my part."

Annabelle looked at me. "Why won't you be there?"

"Vivian's art show is that same night, and I'm planning to go to it with her." There. I'd finally said it out loud. I knew Ruth would be disappointed if I wasn't at the play, but they didn't really need me. My job was finished now. Anyway, I'd feel left out sitting in the audience while everyone else performed.

"I ... um ..." Annabelle shuffled from one foot to the other. "I think Andrew really wants you to be here for the show."

The last person I wanted to talk about with Annabelle was Andrew. And I had no idea why she'd say something like this about Andrew and me, when she so obviously liked him.

She dug her toe in the dirt. "When I first got here, all he could talk about was you. And then something happened—I don't know what. I just want him to be happy again."

She looked up at me, and her smile was gone. All the brightness was gone from her face, actually. I could see clearly how much she cared about Andrew—probably a mirror of my own expression. We stared at each other for a full minute, not saying anything, as understanding passed between us. We both liked Andrew. We both wanted him to be happy. Strange.

"Just think about it," Annabelle said. "If you're here, then you should be in the last dance too. Even Penny's going to be in it. I know having you there would ... mean a lot ... to Andrew."

Through all of this, I hadn't spoken. Now I forced myself to say, "I'll think about it."

I didn't want to think about staying for the show. But even if Annabelle was wrong about whether or not Andrew would care if I were here, I knew that my being here mattered to Ruth. And also to Annabelle, in her own way. So I really would think about it.

But for now, I just wanted to paint.

From: Sadie Douglas
To: Frankie Paulson
Date: Friday, April 27, 6:32 PM
Subject: RE: Call?

Sure, I'll call you tomorrow night after I finish working on the sets so we can work out the details. I can't wait to talk to you!

Chapter 29

Promise

You'll never finish this today." Ruth shook her head as she compared the plans to the faint sketches on the wood. "Good thing my mom said I can stay and help."

I gave Ruth a small paintbrush and asked her to start working on the storefront windowpanes. After a few minutes, I went over to check her work, worried that she'd have trouble with the lines. But it turned out that even though Ruth couldn't draw to save her life, she had a perfectly steady hand with a paintbrush.

She pulled the brush down in one long, steady stroke, biting her lip as she worked.

"Ruth, that's perfect," I said.

The storefronts needed a little flair here and there, but mostly they were time-intensive because of all the borders, which needed straight edges.

"Why didn't you tell me you could paint perfectly straight lines?"

"I didn't know," Ruth said, laughing as she picked her brush up off the board. "So this is going to help?"

"So much," I said. "Dad's picking me up at four o'clock. When do you have to go?"

"Mom is shopping with the twins and said she'd pick me up around two. It's noon now, so I'll call and ask her to come a little later."

After Ruth called her mom, she came back with her iPod and Penny's portable speaker from the office. Once she was sure Cameron had gone for the day, she pulled up her favorite playlist, and the two of us sang along as loudly as we could. I almost didn't want to talk. Right now, singing with Ruth, I could pretend everything that had happened these past few weeks was all in my imagination. Ruth and Andrew and I were all just like we'd been before, Frankie hadn't moved, Mom was getting healthier all the time at the spa, and Vivian was working in her art studio. I could pretend my life hadn't collapsed around me.

"Thanks for watching my dance," Ruth said, breaking the silence between songs.

"You're amazing," I said.

She tossed me a you-don't-have-to-say-that smile and started singing along with the next song.

"Why don't you ever sing for Cameron?" I started on the bakery sign's gold lettering.

"Singing used to be my own thing," Ruth said. "And

then, I met Cam. Since he's got the band, it just seemed weird to sing for him. I mean, if I sang for him and he didn't like my voice and then … you know? Whoops!"

She'd been gesturing with her paintbrush and white drops had fallen onto the door. "I'll fix that, don't worry." She went to look for the brown paint.

"It's over there," I said, pointing to a cup on the table.

She brought the cup back with another brush and a paper towel. She rubbed off as much white as she could and started painting over it with the brown.

"You can't keep your voice a secret from him forever."

"Yes, but it's blown out of proportion. Cam really wants to hear my voice because people have told him I can sing, and now I'm afraid I'll disappoint him. If he'd just accidentally heard me sing once a long time ago, it would be no big deal. You know what I mean?"

I finished the last gold swirl on the old-fashioned E at the end of *Shoppe*, and dunked my brush in the water bucket.

"Yeah. I guess the longer you don't talk about something, the harder it is."

"Speaking of …" Ruth said, cleaning her own brush. "Have you and Andrew talked?"

"Sort of." If an argument counted as a conversation.

Ruth went back to her white windowpanes, and I moved on to the lamps, which I'd drawn to look like iron lanterns hanging off the buildings.

After a few more minutes, Ruth said, "Annabelle told me you're thinking about going to New York next weekend."

"I was going to tell you——"

"Oh, no. It's okay. I'm not saying you shouldn't go … It's just that I agree with her—Andrew would want you to be here."

I stopped painting. "You talked about me and Andrew? With Annabelle?"

She stopped painting and looked up at me, her eyes wide with worry. "It wasn't like that. She said she thinks Andrew is upset and that maybe he misses you. She's worried that by being here, she's causing problems for him. I think last year, when she got sick, maybe she felt more for him than he felt for her. I didn't realize she had those kind of feelings for him, or I would have said something …" her voice trailed off, and I could see she felt like she was digging herself a hole.

I wasn't sure how to help her out of it. "Ruth …"

Ruth sighed. "Now it's my turn. It's not okay, not really. Isn't that what you said to me? I'm really sorry, Sadie."

Suddenly, the whole conversation seemed ridiculous. Ruth and I were tiptoeing around each other as though we were both made of glass. "You don't have to keep apologizing for everything."

"Sor——" Ruth began and then stopped.

I grinned at her, and she grinned back. Suddenly, I remembered painting with Frankie just a few weeks ago. I dipped a finger in the paint bucket and drew a streak down Ruth's forehead and nose.

"Wha——" Ruth started, and then she dipped her own finger in paint and returned the favor.

Soon, we were flipping paint back and forth and laughing

for real. Who cared if the doors were a little splattered? Ruth was back.

"So are you? Going to New York, I mean?" Ruth asked, as we wiped off our hands and faces with paper towels.

Ruth kept her head down, focusing harder than necessary on the towel in her hands. Of course she didn't want me to see her expression. She knew if I saw her face, I'd see how much she wanted me to stay, to watch her in the show; but she wanted me to decide on my own, for my own reasons.

"I'm not sure," I finally said, because I didn't want to lie to her anymore. "I really want to see Frankie, and it sounds nice to get away ... from everything. But I don't know. When I saw you dance, I started thinking maybe I do want to be here. For you. Not for Andrew or Annabelle or anyone else. But for you."

She looked up at me, finally, and I saw the expression in her eyes that I'd expected: A mixture of hope and hurt and sadness.

"I feel ..."

"Sad," I finished for her. "I know. I am too."

"Can I teach you the dance?" she asked as she set down her towel. "Just in case? I promise it won't take long."

I raised my eyebrows at her. "I'm not much of a dancer."

"I'm not much of a painter, and look what I just did." She pointed to the finished windowpanes and then reached out a hand to help me to my feet.

I put my brushes in the water to soak and then grabbed her hand. "Just promise to go slow."

192

Chapter 30

Catch the Wind

"No barking when I'm on the phone, Higgins." I was going to use the hands-free earpiece for our phone so I could cut out leaves for Vivian's art piece while I talked to Frankie. Higgins sat next to me with his tail wagging and his tongue hanging out. "I'm serious," I said sternly, but he only wagged his tail harder.

I scratched his ears and dialed Frankie's number.

"Hello!" Georgiana's voice trilled.

Even over the phone she was overwhelming. I paused mid-cut to form my response. "Um, hi, Georgiana. It's Sadie."

"Sadie, darling! Frankie is expecting your call. And I hear you're coming to stay with us again." Georgiana's heels clicked and I imagined her striding up the stairs and down the hall to Frankie's room.

"Yeah, well, um, maybe," I said.

"Here she is, darling."

"Hey, Sadie."

In the background, Georgiana said, "Say hello, not hey, Francesca. Manners."

"Tell me you're coming to see me," Frankie said as Georgiana's footsteps faded away.

"Still bad, huh?" I liked watching the leaves pile up, glad that Ruth and Bea and Lindsay were now cutting out leaves too. Maybe, fingers crossed, we might finish enough of them before Vivian had to leave for New York.

"You know, she never gets mad at me. No matter what I do, she always uses that same tone of voice. If she'd just yell once in a while ... "

"Vivian is almost finished with the exhibit. Dad went over to help her with the cement pour, and I guess she's been working round the clock. We're helping with the leaves." I waved one for emphasis. "I'm cutting them out right now."

"I want to help too," Frankie said.

"Perfect! I'll send you fabric and wire, express mail, so you can glue them into strands of ivy. We need at least a thousand more."

"Who else is helping?"

I sighed. "Ruth, Bea, and Lindsay."

"So," Frankie said. "You okay?"

"No," I admitted. "I should be okay. I mean, I worked things out with Ruth, and I understand now why everyone was protecting Annabelle ... I should be happy but I'm just not."

"How's your mom?" Frankie asked.

"Not good."

Frankie waited and I continued to cut, wondering what I wanted to say. Finally I said, "I'm afraid I'm going to be like this — crazy — for the rest of my life. Every time I think I've worked my life out, it falls apart again."

I could feel Frankie thinking across the phone line, and then she said, "Do you remember the church we went to on Easter Sunday? And what the pastor said?"

"Yeah, who could forget?"

"I think she's right, about life being a series of transformations. I've been thinking about that a lot lately. My life keeps going up and down and up again. Sometimes when I draw, I feel hopeful. You told me those tiny moments of hope matter, remember? But there doesn't seem to be one fix-everything experience."

I remembered how I'd felt swinging with Frankie. I'd known that life couldn't stay so good forever, but I'd wanted to hold on to that feeling of being fully happy. Maybe I was trying so hard to hold myself together that I'd kept myself from both the bad and the good. Maybe I couldn't get back to being happy if I didn't let myself fall apart a little too.

"Did you know that a caterpillar totally disintegrates inside its cocoon before reshaping itself into a butterfly?" Frankie asked.

I smiled into the phone. "How'd you get so smart?"

"About butterflies?" she asked.

"I thought I was helping *you* with the whole scavenger hunt thing. Turns out you're the one helping me."

"I should listen to my own advice," Frankie said. "It's a lot easier to help everyone else."

I laughed. "No kidding."

"So ... are you coming to New York?" Frankie asked.

"Maybe," I said. "I want to."

"I want you to, too," she said.

I finished a leaf and set it down. "I think I need to draw now, Frankie."

"Okay," she said. "I'll be drawing too."

I hung up the phone and took out my sketchbook, turning to the picture of the locked box. I hesitated.

Do I really have to?

The picture stared at me from the page, fresh and clear: A messy knot hidden away inside a locked box. The key to the box, just waiting to be used.

It's time.

One time, Pips and I had gone to a rock-climbing wall and climbed all the way to the top. To get down, you had to lean back and let go, letting the rope hold your weight as you kicked off from the wall. Turning to a blank page and, opening myself up to what was inside that locked box, felt like letting go at the top of that wall. Would the rope hold me?

I started to draw—quickly, so I wouldn't think too much. First, I drew myself. I was caught in a net, but busily untangling it, trying to free myself. I turned to the next page in the sketchbook, knowing that something bigger was about to come—willing something bigger to come. Mom's face came first, and then her body, curled up, motionless in a net just like mine—only her net had trapped her.

I turned the page, hoping for a new image. I couldn't stop Mom from being tangled up. Nothing I did or said would make any difference. Like the wind, I couldn't control anything that happened outside of me—I couldn't even control how I felt about it. I could only control my own choices. I thought about Ruth, about the way she'd looked when I'd watched her dance.

On the next page, Mom appeared again. But this time, she stood facing the ocean, her arms flung wide. I stood beside her in exactly the same stance. We'd stood this way many times before back in California, trying to catch the wind. Since we'd lived so close to the ocean, we'd go to the beach two or three times a month, rain or shine.

Mom would say, "Sades, let's go catch the wind," and we'd pile into the car, just Mom and me.

She could still catch the wind, even though she was sick. But even if we lived in California now, she wasn't likely to lean across the table and look at me with that old sparkle in her eye. In a way, I understood now, having felt darkness press down on me, making me feel like I'd rather lie in bed all day rather than do just about anything. But I also knew that the only way out of the darkness was to give something—even something small. I needed Mom, and maybe she'd forgotten that.

I'd forgotten—or maybe I just hadn't realized—that

Vivian needed me. Viv and I had promised one another that no matter what, we'd give everything to our art, pouring all of the exhaustion, anger, loneliness, and fear into something outside ourselves. We weren't pretending to be perfect; but knowing that if nothing else, we were giving one another a gift. And we helped each other simply by keeping our promise.

Yes. The word rippled through me. *Yes.*

I'd pretended with Mom for a very long time. But maybe it was time for me to tell her how much I needed her.

I set down my sketchbook, took a deep breath, and headed down the hall to Mom's bedroom.

Chapter 31

Don't Give Up

Mom lay on her side, her hair deep red against the white pillowcase. Her fingers curled around the edge of the comforter, holding it close the way a small child might hold a blanket. Her eyes were closed, the lashes a dark fringe against her pale cheeks. I didn't know if she was awake, asleep, or someplace in between. Only a sliver of light came through the closed curtains.

I stepped into the darkened room, which smelled of the violets Dad had left on the bedside table.

"Mom?" I whispered.

When she didn't answer, I went to sit next to her on the bed and took her hand in mine. Her skin was soft, and her hand felt like a baby bird—delicate and so fragile.

"Mom," I whispered again, and her eyelashes fluttered open.

"Sadie," she said, her voice thick with sleep.

I tried to picture her standing on the beach with her arms outstretched, not curled up inside the net. Everything inside of me wanted to slip back into Mom-Sadie mode, where I pretended everything was okay, and she did too.

She needs to know she has something to give.

"Mom, I need your help." I set her hand back down on the comforter and pulled my legs in close to my chin.

She blinked a few times, breathed deep, and pushed herself up on the pillows, as if entering the room for the first time. "What did you say?"

"I messed up everything with Ruth and Andrew. It's a long, complicated story. And now I've tried to fix things with Ruth at least, but ... I still feel ..." My voice trailed off. I hated the sound of the word in my head.

"Lonely," she said.

It had been a long time since Mom could finish any sentence for me.

"Yes. When everything went wrong, I fell apart. And then I felt like I was in this fog, this darkness that I couldn't get out of. I didn't mean to act badly, but I couldn't help it."

Mom took my hand. "Oh, Sadie."

I didn't know how to ask, so I just let the words out. "Is that how you feel?"

Mom looked down at the comforter, twisting it between her fingers. Finally, she said. "It's not the sickness, it's the other thing, the stronger thing. Loneliness, sadness — like you said, darkness."

"When Frankie moved away, I told her I thought the hard parts of life were worth it because in the hard times, you learn that God is with you. But then Vivian's house flooded, and Annabelle came and you—"

"I let you down," Mom finished.

"You're sick," I said, shaking my head.

"I'm not just sick," Mom said. "We both know I could be better than I am."

We sat in silence for a while, while my words burned inside me, aching to be said. If I spoke them, I'd cross the invisible divide we'd had in place for so long. I'd be admitting I couldn't do this by myself. In some ways, these words were harder to say than "I love you." They couldn't be taken back.

"I need you, Mom."

She didn't answer right away, and the hollowness began to settle in again. Maybe I'd been wrong. I never should have come to Mom's room, never should have risked saying—

"I need you too, Sadie," Mom finally said. "Not the way you try to be—strong and perfect—but like this. I need to be your mom."

I looked into her clear green eyes and realized I couldn't remember the last time I'd looked at her—really looked. Or the last time I'd let her look at me. But now she looked at me, into me, as though she wasn't seeing only my face, but my heart too. Layers peeled away inside of me until I felt totally exposed, no more shield. I let Mom see my numbness, my fear.

"I'm afraid I'm never going to be okay," I said. "That no matter what, I'm going to keep falling apart."

Mom pulled me close and stroked my hair. "I've watched you, Sadie, ever since we moved here. You're so fiercely committed to finding the truth, to doing what's right, to being a loyal friend. But no matter how hard you try, you can't help but fall apart sometimes. That's when you need people to love you, to help you put yourself back together, to get stronger. You're the one who taught me that, actually. I've forgotten these past few weeks that falling apart isn't the end."

I felt like I was in a dream again, lying there in Mom's arms the way I used to do when I was small. "Remember that time when I walked in and you were praying?"

"Yes." I heard the smile in Mom's voice. "I scared you that day."

"Do you think it's possible to be friends with God?" I asked.

"Absolutely. I believe God wants to be as close to us as our next breath," Mom said. "I think most times we hold him at a distance because we're afraid. But God is bigger than our fear."

"But what about when he lets us down, like—"

"Like when he doesn't make me better, no matter how much we all try?" Mom finished.

I closed my eyes against the tears, but they ran down my cheeks anyway. "Yes. Why doesn't he just heal you? Why did he let you get sick in the first place?"

"I wonder that myself, Sades. All the time. And I don't

have any good answers. But I do know that God is still here with me. I hear him, even on my darkest days—even when I'm trying not to."

"What's the answer then? What are we supposed to do?"

"Honestly? I think life is about finding the right questions to ask, because questions move us forward, they cause us to seek and wonder. Answers are only temporary, and when we think we've found them, we often stop in our tracks."

"So if you believe all this, how come ..."

"I forget too, Sades. And I need you and Dad and God to remind me. Some days it's hard not to give up."

"Please don't give up," I whispered.

She kissed the top of my head, and we sat like that for a while longer. I felt the knots untangling inside of me. I may not have the answers, but I did have questions. And I had Mom. And Dad. And Ruth. Pips and Frankie. And the voice in the dark. I had God.

Mom handed me a tissue. "Now what's this I hear about you going back to New York?"

I dried my cheeks. "I want to go to Vivian's art show and visit Frankie, but I mostly want to go so I won't have to be here to watch the play. And Annabelle."

"But ... ?"

"But Annabelle said Andrew wants me to see the show. And I know Ruth wants me to be here too. Not just *wants* me to be here, but my being here will mean something to them. I mean, Frankie wants to see me too. But I feel like, after everything that's happened, I owe it to Ruth to watch her in the show."

Mom stroked my cheek and smiled. "Something tells me you'll have the answer for this one very soon."

I hugged her tight. "Thanks, Mom."

From downstairs Dad called, "Spaghetti, anyone?"

Mom and I walked downstairs, hand in hand.

Chapter 32

Being There

Andrew stepped out of the trees in his king costume, crossed to the bakery door, and watched Annabelle as she sang and danced. A small smile played around his lips, sending a sharp pang through me. He didn't have to act to look that way, to have that mixture of satisfaction, pride, and happiness when he looked at Annabelle. He might say it was because he was so happy she'd come so far since last year. And maybe that was even true. His scene was short, but he was still having trouble with his lines.

I caught Ruth watching me, and I felt another stab. But now I didn't know what I felt. Sadness? Guilt? Confusion, mostly. I hoped Mom was right and I'd just know what to do about New York. Or maybe the problem was that I wasn't being honest with myself. I *did* know what I should do, but I wasn't sure I *could*.

"When were you planning to memorize this?" Penny interrupted Andrew. "We open the show on Friday. Less than a week from today."

"I'm sorry," Andrew said. "I promise I'll have it down by tomorrow."

"All right. We'll come back to this scene tomorrow. For now, let's move on to the dance."

This was the moment of truth. I'd promised Penny, on pain of death, that I'd decide about being in the play by the time we practiced this final dance today. She wanted to set everyone's positions today, so if she added me to the dance, everyone would be thrown off if I didn't show up for the real thing. I swallowed hard.

"Sadie, are you dancing?" Penny called.

I glanced back at Ruth. I'd promised Vivian I wouldn't pretend. I wouldn't try to be perfect, or try to make everyone else happy. The answer grew inside me, rolling over and up as though tossed by the waves, coming closer to the surface all the time. Finally, I opened my mouth and the answer tumbled from my lips.

"Yes."

Penny raised an eyebrow. "It's a final answer, you know. No changing your mind?"

"Right," I said, nodding.

Annabelle let out a shriek of happiness and ran over to hug me. I caught Andrew watching us with a surprised look. When she let go of me, Ruth hugged me too.

"Thank you, Sadie," Annabelle said. "This means so much to me, I can't even tell you."

"I didn't want you to have to work that music box all on your own," I said, doing my best to return her smile.

I could still feel Andrew watching us as we lined up for the dance. As the music started, I was surprised that instead of watching Annabelle, he kept watching me. When I looked up and caught his eye, he smiled very slightly and turned away. But not before I noticed that the tips of his ears were bright red.

After the dance and the curtain call, I went back to the set station to make sure there was nothing left to do. Tomorrow's rehearsal was our last one before the show, and I didn't want any surprises.

I cleaned the paintbrushes and capped the paint cans. Doug and Penny had promised to help me carry all of the supplies back inside before tomorrow's rehearsal.

"Sadie?" Andrew said from behind me.

My heart stopped for a fraction of a second before it started beating again, faster than before. I turned to face him.

"Would you help me with my lines tonight?" he asked. "I can't do it on my own."

"Can't Annabelle help you?" I asked before I could stop myself.

"Her family has already moved over to the lake house," Andrew said. "And she's busy with her own lines, anyway. And ..."

"And what?" I asked.

"And I ..."

For one crazy second, I thought he was going to hug me,

the way he used to. But the moment passed and he stepped back, shrugging.

"You what?" I asked.

"I think you'd be a lot of help," he said with a false ring to his words.

"That isn't what you were going to say, is it?" I asked.

"No." His lips curled up into the smile I loved, the smile I didn't think I'd ever see again. "So, will you?"

I shrugged but couldn't help smiling. "Sure. I guess so."

Dad drove me over to the research cabin, and I could hardly sit still.

"Call when you're ready for me to pick you up," Dad said as I closed the Jeep door.

"Love you, Dad," I said, my arms full of green fabric.

I still had to cut out leaves in every spare second. Vivian would leave for New York in a few days, and I still had about three hundred leaves to go.

Andrew and I decided to sit on the porch, so I set up my pile of fabric and started cutting while he turned to his page in the script.

"Memorization isn't my thing," he said.

"Let's go through it slowly," I said.

He started reciting his first line, and I saw right away what the problem was. "Andrew, you're so worried about saying the exact words on the page, you're not thinking about what you're saying."

I suggested that before he tried memorizing them as they're written, he should try paraphrasing his lines until he knew what each one was about.

208

"Wow, it's so much easier now." He grinned at me. "Amazing!"

"So now you can help me cut out leaves," I said.

"Let's take a break first." Andrew helped me up. "How about a game of Sink the Log? Last one there has to cut out the rest of the leaves."

He took off running.

"No fair!" I called after him, laughing. "You're such a cheater!"

I sprinted to catch up, but he was so far ahead of me that he reached the creek a full fifteen seconds before I did.

"Didn't you say the first person who gets here has to cut out the rest of the leaves?" I asked.

"Nice try." Andrew winked at me. "But maybe I'll still help you out of the goodness of my heart."

He tossed a stick into the water, and we gathered up some rocks to throw to try to sink it. Some of my rocks hit the stick, but most of them plunked into the water. Soon, the stick was out of view.

"Rematch." I looked for another good stick.

Andrew caught my arm. "I wish you'd wear your necklace."

I stopped and looked up at him. "I didn't think ..."

"I'm sorry for what I said," Andrew said. "I was worried about Annabelle, and confused about you. You weren't acting like yourself, and I started to wonder — if I still felt the same way about you."

"You used to be my best friend," I said, and then realized I wasn't exactly telling the truth. "And more. But now ..."

"I'm not asking for everything to be exactly like it was right this minute," Andrew said. "But I hope it will be again—someday."

My stomach flip-flopped, and I couldn't look him in the eye without blushing. I pulled my arm away and grabbed the first stick I saw.

"Now for real," I said. "Rematch!"

We ran around gathering rocks. A rustle in the bushes stopped me.

"Andrew, stop," I whispered, pointing across the creek.

July and her two cubs stepped out of the underbrush and came down to the water to drink. We sat on the bank watching the two cubs splash in the water until July huffed at them and turned to go. The white cub looked me in the eyes once more, almost exactly the same way she had just a few weeks before.

"Incredible," Andrew said when the bears had gone.

"I know." We stayed still, listening to the crickets until the sun slipped behind the trees.

From: Sadie Douglas
To: Frankie Paulson
Date: Sunday, April 29, 8:20 PM
Subject: New York

Frankie, I can't come visit you this time. I'm so sorry. But Mom promised to drive me to New York at least one more time before we move back to California so I can see you. And I have an idea for this weekend that I think you'll like. Look for a note in the box that I'm going to send with Vivian. She'll be there on Wednesday, so you'll have a few days to help with the leaves and ivy, if you want to.

Chapter 33

By the Light of the Moon

With finishing Vivian's leaves and seeing her off to New York, play rehearsals and paint touch-ups, ticket sales and other preparations, the week flew by.

Finally, Friday night arrived. I slipped into my costume: black leggings, a black T-shirt, black socks, and black shoes. I'd wear this for the majority of the show while I helped Annabelle with the music box backstage, and then I'd add a ballet skirt over the top for the final dance. I checked my reflection in the mirror and decided to go for it. I took Andrew's necklace out of my dresser drawer, put it on, and hurried out of my room before I could change my mind.

I gave Higgins an extra treat as we went out the door. "We'll be back soon, Higgy."

Dad helped Mom into the Jeep, and I took the backseat.

"We're so proud of you," Dad said as he pulled out onto the road.

I laughed. "Wait till you see my dancing before you decide how proud you are of me."

Stars appeared one by one in the deepening sky. We'd decided to do the entire show by moonlight and tiki torch, particularly because tonight was a full moon and there would be plenty of light.

Dad pulled into the parking lot and Mom gave me a hug, handing me her iPhone. "Take good care of it."

I hurried off to the Tree House where the cast was gathering while the audience assembled. I checked the time. Seven-fifteen. Perfect.

I climbed the rope ladder to the Tree House. Ruth, Annabelle, Bea, Lindsay, and Andrew were all waiting.

"You guys ready?" I asked.

They gathered around me as I dialed Vivian's cell phone number. Vivian's face appeared in the screen. "Hey, guys!"

"Say hello, not hey," Georgiana trilled in the background. Then she said, "Oops! I thought that was Frankie. Sorry, Vivian!"

We all laughed as Vivian passed the phone to Frankie.

"How's it going?" I asked.

Frankie panned the phone around the room to show off the forest filled with sculptures and the ivy-covered piano. "It's perfect," she said. "And people have been adding their memories to the ivy all night."

She walked over to give us a closer look at the ivy. The leaves were covered with gold letters, words symbolizing the memories left behind by the people who'd visited the exhibit already.

"Are you ready?" Frankie asked.

I gathered everyone close. Frankie opened the envelope we'd sent, with each of our memories written in gold. One by one, Frankie added them to the ivy strands on the piano.

"I wish you were here," she said when she'd finished.

"We wish you were here too," I said.

"Break a leg tonight," she said.

"We will!" we all answered, and then we waved good-bye.

Penny gathered us for a pre-show prayer before we went out to the moonlit stages.

"Sadie, will you pray for us?" she asked.

Goosebumps prickled across my skin as I nodded. I'd never prayed out loud for the group before. We all closed our eyes.

"God, you are with us always—when we know you're there, and when we forget. Thank you. Please be with us tonight, too, as we tell your story. Help us to be giving and loving and to always seek the truth. In your name ..."

"Amen." Everyone said with me.

"Let's go do this thing," Doug said.

We all laughed and headed out into the moonlight.

THE END

We want to hear from you. Please send your comments about this book to us in care of zreview@zondervan.com. Thank you.